continued on next page . . .

TOME
OF DEATH

D. R. MEREDITH

BERKLEY PRIME CRIME, NEW YORK

THE BERKLEY PUBLISHING GROUP
Published by the Penguin Group
Penguin Group (USA) Inc.
375 Hudson Street, New York, New York 10014, USA

Penguin Group (Canada), 10 Alcorn Avenue, Toronto, Ontario M4V 3B2, Canada
(a division of Pearson Penguin Canada Inc.)
Penguin Books Ltd., 80 Strand, London WC2R 0RL, England
Penguin Group Ireland, 25 St. Stephen's Green, Dublin 2, Ireland (a division of Penguin Books Ltd.)
Penguin Group (Australia), 250 Camberwell Road, Camberwell, Victoria 3124, Australia
(a division of Pearson Australia Group Pty. Ltd.)
Penguin Books India Pvt. Ltd., 11 Community Centre, Panchsheel Park, New Delhi—110 017, India
Penguin Group (NZ), Cnr. Airborne and Rosedale Roads, Albany, Auckland 1310, New Zealand
(a division of Pearson New Zealand Ltd.)
Penguin Books (South Africa) (Pty.) Ltd., 24 Sturdee Avenue, Rosebank, Johannesburg 2196, South
Africa

Penguin Books Ltd., Registered Offices: 80 Strand, London WC2R 0RL, England

This is a work of fiction. Names, characters, places, and incidents either are the product of the author's imagination or are used fictitiously, and any resemblance to actual persons, living or dead, business establishments, events, or locales is entirely coincidental.

TOME OF DEATH

A Berkley Prime Crime Book / published by arrangement with the author

PRINTING HISTORY
Berkley Prime Crime mass-market edition / February 2005

Copyright © 2005 by Doris R. Meredith.
Cover design by Rita Frangie.
Cover art by Chris O'Leary.

ISBN: 0-425-18274-6

Berkley Prime Crime Books are published by The Berkley Publishing Group,
a division of Penguin Group (USA) Inc.,
375 Hudson Street, New York, New York 10014.
The name BERKLEY PRIME CRIME and the BERKLEY PRIME CRIME design
are trademarks belonging to Penguin Group (USA) Inc.

PRINTED IN THE UNITED STATES OF AMERICA

10 9 8 7 6 5 4 3 2 1

Any resemblance between my characters and any persons actually living in Amarillo, Texas, is coincidental and utterly unintentional. Personalities of actual historical figures mentioned are based on biographies and extensive research. The events portrayed are a figment of my imagination and not meant to mirror actual events, past or present.

—D. R. MEREDITH

ACKNOWLEDGMENTS

The Coffee House Gals
Who Meet the First Tuesday of Every Month
For Purposes of Literary Discussion
and a Bit of Female Conversation

Melissa Lockman, Lanoma Beatty, Pamela Pool Barnes,
Gayle Slaughter, Chris Ferguson, Jeannette Wedding,
Carolyn Canon, Janie Thomas, Mary Whitton, Jan Bell,
Kim Sterling, and Yours Truly, D. R. Meredith

Hieronymus Bosch
1986–2003
A Beloved Beagle, the Inspiration for Rembrandt,
and Family Member of Fur
Rest in Peace, Old Friend

Nérmernuh
Nurmurnuh

AUTHOR'S NOTES

The People who became the Comanche were first called the Snake people, or Shoshoné. Perhaps because they once lived near the Snake River, where they existed in small bands of hunters-gatherers, and the long, cold winters killed the young and the old, while those between survived at a starvation level. They are believed to once be part of the present day Shoshoné who, for whatever reason, broke away, migrated from the mountains to the Great Plains and south to the lands of Kansas, Texas, southeastern Colorado, and eastern New Mexico. Their origin—beyond the fact that they, like other Amerindians, emigrated from Asia—is shrouded in the mists of prehistory. They had few myths, folklore, or rituals. They vaguely remembered tribal lore that said they sprang from a mating of the animals; primarily the wolf, whom they revered. Therefore, there was a taboo against killing the wolf and its four-legged cousins: the coyote and the dog.

The Comanche called themselves Nérmernuh, which means "true human beings." All tribes had their own name for themselves, and every name meant "People." Each tribe of "People" believed themselves to be more human than any other. It was a form of ethnocentric behavior that arose from a time when small populations lived isolated from other tribes in a vast, empty continent. When one lives separately from other human beings, one tends to believe that your ways are best. It is a trait of all human cultures.

In 1705, Spanish settlers in New Mexico met the nemesis of their aspirations for further empire building when a tribe of Mountain Utes appeared, accompanied by a band of dark, squat Amerindians the Utes identified as "Koha-mahts," meaning "Those Who Are Always Against Us." History would know them as the Comanche, who adopted the horse in the latter part of the seventeenth century and became the most powerful, most cunning. most feared, and most successful horse Indians of the Great Plains. They were superb buffalo hunters and warriors, who prevented the Spanish from conquering the American West as far north as Canada; stood between the French and their hopes of moving into the Southwest; and for sixty years stopped the Anglo-American settlement of the land the Comanche controlled. They rode down from the north, a short, dark race, barrel-chested with heavily muscled arms and slim, almost bandy legs, and they conquered the imagination of white Americans as the finest horsemen and most vicious warriors in the world, before riding into history, still as mysterious at their finale as a culture as they were when first seen by the Spanish.

When you meet Spotted Tongue, Fat Belly, Shaking Hand, and Green Willow, do not judge them by today's standards. They were warriors and lived by the code of the warrior. They were Comanches, stone-age people whose culture was as different from that of twenty-first century Americans as can be imagined. Stealing horses, raiding settlements and isolated cabins, rape, murder, and the taking of captives were not crimes to them, but acceptable behavior. War was a way of life. Their behavior differs very little from that of any army of any conqueror in history: the Egyptian Pharaohs, Alexander the Great, the Roman Caesars, Genghis Khan, William the Conqueror, the Christians and the Moslems during the Crusades, and the Spanish Conquistadores, to name a few. Many an enemy village was put the torch—after being looted, of course, and the maidens ravished—during the endless European wars of past centuries. Where the Old World and the New World differed radically was what T.H. Fehrenbach calls the Amerindians' world view. The Amerindians, including the Comanches, saw the world as ruled by random chance and magic. They did not recognize cause and effect. One must utilize magic to succeed in the world. When Spotted Tongue loses his ability to "make medicine," he believes he loses the ability to protect himself against bad luck. The Comanche, in common with other Amerindians, saw magic as a substitute for science and experience a substitute for observation. Altering the world view of any society begins with the change in one person's perception, for whatever reason, of how the world works. Spotted Tongue is that one person. His perception changes when he learns that medicine or the lack of it doesn't alter events. This knowledge makes him different, and in a society as conservative as the Comanche, being different could be as dangerous as being a Quaker in Puritan New England.

The Comanches spoke a dialect of the Uto-Aztekan language group which, of course, is rendered as English in the narrative. If all the Comanche characters are speaking the same language—rendered into English—then sprinkling random Comanche phrases which require translation needlessly interrupts both the narrative flow and the suspension of disbelief. Plus, the phrases would be redundant. The only Comanche words used are "Nermernuh," meaning

True Human Beings, or People; and "Nerm," meaning Human Being. "Nermernuh" and "People" are used interchangeably in the narrative. Spotted Tongue showing Little Flower the scalps he has taken during the last raid in Texas demonstrates that he is a powerful Comanche warrior more clearly than any number of Comanche phrases. Spotted Tongue is capable of love and hate, friendship and loyalty, sadness and grief, but he also takes scalps. He is not a romanticized movie Indian. He is not Tonto. He is Spotted Tongue, Comanche warrior—and reluctant detective.

PROLOGUE

PALO DURO CANYON, 1868

Spotted Tongue sprawled on a blanket under a brush arbor—buffalo skin tipis only being used during the time when freezing winds blew—staring through the loosely woven roof at the sky and sweating in the heat. Brush arbors straggled along the bank of the narrow stream, each one far enough from the next not to block the breezes that dried the sweat caused by the fierce sun, a sun so hot that it bleached the sky a pale blue. A faint haze of very fine dust still hung over the valley floor from last night's dancing of warriors and their women celebrating a successful raid. What grass was left after days of cook fires, the running feet of children and dogs, and the occasional ponies ridden through the middle of the camp, grew along the edges of the stream.

Spotted Tongue had chosen not to go on the raid. He

*had noticed the surprised looks of Shaking Hand and Wild
Horse. He always went on raids, and he usually led them as
war chief. This time Coyote Dung had taken his place.
Only his closest friend wasn't surprised. Fat Belly believed
Spotted Tongue stayed behind because his white mare was
due to foal, and he didn't want to leave such a valuable
pony to the mercies of his Mexican slaves. Spotted Tongue
owned the only white horse in the Peoples's huge pony
herd. The other men believed that Spotted Tongue captured
the white mare last year because his medicine was strong.
Good things came to those who possessed strong medicine.*

*Spotted Tongue knew it was not his medicine. He had
possessed no medicine during the raid when he stole the
white mare, nor any since then. Not that he hadn't tried. He
had walked by himself into the prairie and stayed for four
days and four nights without food, imploring the spirit that
lived in the wolf to send him a vision. But he had seen no
vision, sensed no spirit. The only result of his quest was a
ferocious hunger. Feeling cold and sick in his belly he went
on the raid anyway, hoping he would not bring bad luck to
the other warriors. He feared the bullet from some Tejano's
gun would enter his breast, and blood would pour from his
mouth and he would die. Instead, he had caught the white
mare. He worried from that day to this, worried until his
head ached as to why, when he had no medicine, good fortune had blessed him. And had blessed him again when he
captured Little Flower.*

*Spotted Tongue dried off his sweaty back on the blanket
and sat up. It was too hot to sleep. He slapped at a fly on
his arm. The heat drew the flies and gnats that bit both the
Nermernuh and the horses. He drew his legs up to rest his
arms on his knees. Without medicine he felt uneasy, as if he
was crossing the river and the sand tried to suck him down.
A warrior without medicine could trust nothing: not his*

horse to carry him without stepping in a prairie dog hole; nor his friends not to betray him; nor the ground beneath his feet to remain solid. He held his secret in his heart, for there was no one to tell, no one from whom to take council. It was the custom of the People that men speak directly to one another from the heart. But even his best friend, Fat Belly, did not understand, but stared at him with fear in his eyes. Spotted Tongue leaned over to rest his head on his arms. How could Fat Belly understand when he, Spotted Tongue, a man of reputed wisdom, did not? And what would Fat Belly say if Spotted Tongue told him that it wasn't worry over the white mare that kept him from the raid, but instead he stayed to protect Little Flower from mistreatment by the other women, behavior no self-respecting warrior would consider. He felt separated from the Nermernuh. And lonely.

He heard the soft sound of moccasins sliding across the grass along the stream bank and leaped to his feet, ducking out of the arbor. He was already gripping his lance when he recognized Green Willow. She was still a pretty woman with only few signs of aging, although she would soon pass her thirtieth winter, as would he. She was a short, sturdy woman with bowed legs and coarse black hair chopped off below her ears as was the custom with women of the People. And like all the People, her face was broad with high cheekbones and dark brown eyes. She wore orange paint on her cheeks and had reddened her ears, again as was common with women. Sweat had streaked through the paint on her cheeks, leaving clear tracks behind. Her skin was copper-colored, lighter than his, but then he only covered his body with a breechclout and moccasins that reached above the knee. The sun turned him dark.

"Don't sneak up on me, Green Willow! I might have thrown my lance through your belly! I have warned you

before. Do I need to beat you before you remember?" he threatened, and a threat was all it was. He could not recall ever beating Green Willow. He had beaten only one woman, and she was not Green Willow.

Spotted Tongue leaned his fourteen-foot lance against the outside of the arbor. Sometimes he thought women lacked the sense of a good horse. A well-trained horse never sneaked up behind a warrior. Another heartbeat and he would have been unable to stop from throwing his lance. He wiped the sweat from his forehead and waited for his heart to slow its beating.

Finally calm, he looked over Green Willow's shoulder, his thick brows drawing together to give his face the ferocious expression he wore when attacking an enemy. "Where is Little Flower? Did you leave her alone with the other women?"

"She was not working hard," said Green Willow, a note of bitterness in her voice that Spotted Tongue could not help hearing. "She thinks that she can do as she pleases. I left her behind in the canyon, gawking at its walls and trees like she had never seen the like before. She is strange, Spotted Tongue; even for a foreigner she is strange. Why don't you kill her, or give her to us women? We would like to have sport with a captive again, especially her. Last night only whetted our appetites." She gasped as he grabbed her wrist with a strong grip.

"I will not kill her, and neither will you! And keep those other women away from her if I am gone from camp." He released Green Willow's arm. His heart was pounding inside his chest with a warning of danger. Something threatened. This is what happens when a warrior has no medicine. He has a pain in his head and his belly and is unable to command his family.

Green Willow rubbed her wrist where Spotted Tongue had grabbed her. "If she does not return with her blanket filled with the wild plums, I will beat her myself. I am your first wife, and she must obey me."

Spotted Tongue grabbed her shoulders. "And you must obey me! You will not touch her. And if she has run away, you will be the one beaten. Do you understand?"

Green Willow nodded her head, her eyes downcast, but he saw the rage and hurt in her eyes and felt ashamed of himself. "I understand," she said, her body rigid.

"I will find her and bring her back," he said, pushing her away in his haste and striding down the canyon toward the enormous horse herd. He did not look back. He did not have to; he could feel Green Willow watching him. She probably hoped the ponies would stampede and run over him. If harm had come to Little Flower, he would hope the same.

PALO DURO CANYON, FIVE YEARS AGO

The woman stood on her balcony watching the shadows of night creep up the walls of the canyon as the sun sank lower in the sky. This was her favorite time of the day, when the blistering sun finally set and the temperature dropped to a more comfortable level. She watched an eagle spiral upward on the updraft caused when hot air rose from the canyon floor. She closed her eyes and listened to the buzzing of the cicada and the not-so-distant yips of the coyote. The plum thickets that lined the dry creek bed on the canyon floor below rustled from the scurrying of small mammals such as rabbits and squirrels, each seeking the ripe plums which had dropped from the bushes. She stood motionless and let the peace of the gathering dusk envelop her. If only she were as happy the rest of the day as she was at sunset.

She waited until full darkness before she turned and entered her house, sliding the glass door shut but not bothering to lock it. No one along the rim of Sunday Canyon locked their doors. While situated on different levels, some balanced on the very rim, others built on ledges on the walls of the canyon itself, the houses were close and few. Most were weekend houses, but lately several occupants were beginning to live in the canyon all year round.

Nowhere was as ruggedly beautiful and as peaceful as this little side canyon that was almost an arroyo when compared to the depths of the larger Palo Duro. But however much she loved the canyon, she must leave it to go back home where she belonged. She would return to the land where rain fell and the rivers and streams ran full, not like the Texas Panhandle where it seldom rained and the summers were hot and dry and the winters fiercely cold when the infrequent blizzards left behind snow drifts chest high. This was an alien land and an alien people to her. She must leave for the sake of her own survival. Only one man held her here and while she did not hate him, she did not love him either—not as much or as deeply as he demanded.

She heard the glass door slide open and whirled around. "What do you want?" she asked, unconsciously backing up as the other person stalked toward her. "We have nothing to say to each other. It's all been said and we'll never agree, so leave me alone. Get out of my house."

Without realizing it she had backed into a corner. She was trapped. She drew a deep breath and held it, flooding her body with oxygen, feeling the rush of adrenalin that prepared her to push the interloper back, back, back, through the door and outside. She stepped forward, her hands outstretched. She caught a glint of the knife just before it sliced across her palm. She uttered a faint scream, jerking her hand back in shock. As she felt the blood trickle, then drip off her hand onto the tile floor, she recognized that she faced death in the person of one she knew as well as she knew the canyon below. She cradled her sliced palm in her other hand, white-hot pain beginning to dull her mind. She felt sweat dampen her denim shirt along with the red drops of blood that dotted the front of the garment. If she lived, she would throw the shirt away.

"Wait! Please! We have to talk!" she cried out, grabbing for her assailant's hand. If she could get the knife, disarm her murderer, she would have a chance to live. But it was too late. She had never fought another person, and she didn't know how to protect herself while striking out. She hardly felt the first hot thrust and certainly didn't feel the subsequent ones. She hardly had time to wonder that she had so misjudged her murderer.

1

The fact that he was desperate to be on a dig hardly meant that he had lost all sense of proportion.

—Gideon Oliver in Aaron Elkins'
Curses, 1989

PALO DURO CANYON, PRESENT DAY

The Murder by the Yard Reading Circle sat on camp stools, lawn chairs, or blankets spread on the ground in the midst of a grove of cottonwood trees. Megan Clark and Ryan Stevens sat in the lawn chairs because Ryan decided they were the most comfortable seats, and he had no intention of squatting on camp stools or sitting cross-legged on blankets which barely provided a pad against the stony ground. "If you had spent as many years sitting on hard auditorium chairs as I have while my fellow professors droned on and on in faculty meetings, you would pick the most comfortable chairs, too," he told Megan. "Why do you think I always sit on the couch whenever we meet at the bookstore?"

Megan ignored his mutterings. Frankly, she would rather be sitting on a camp stool. The vinyl weave of the lawn chair was imprinting itself on her bare legs. She would have to peel herself out of the chair when the reading circle's discussion was over and it was time for the group hike. Well, not exactly a group hike, more like a leisurely walk given the fact that some members of the reading circle were a little on the elderly side. Rosemary Pittman and Lorene Getz, for example. Megan wasn't quite sure how old the two ladies were, but both had white hair the texture of cotton candy and lines and creases on their faces that told of a full life. Megan felt uneasy thinking of the two ladies she always referred to as "The Twins" because of their similar appearance as actually being old. She liked elderly people, or anything else old for that matter, but she didn't like to think that the Twins were closer to their funerals than to their births. Which was a ridiculous sentiment for an archaeologist used to old, dead artifacts. Although to be specific, her degree was in physical anthropology with specialties in paleopathology and human osteology—which meant she performed autopsies on mummies and prehistoric or extinct human species, or examined bones if the remains were past the mummy stage—which explained why she was an assistant reference librarian. There weren't too many mummies to autopsy, and when one turned up, at least fifty paleopathologists—or bioarchaeologists if you preferred that term—were in line ahead of her. Sometimes she thought she should go to work as a curator in a museum somewhere instead of waiting for the opportunity to go on a dig where a mummy was likely to turn up. But the mummies in museums had for the most part already been sliced, diced, and examined under the microscope. What they ate, what they wore, and what diseases cursed their lives were no longer secrets. What she wouldn't have given to be part of the team who studied the Ice Man, the Iron Age gentleman found frozen in the Alps, a mummy about whom paleopathologists could ask questions that had no answers yet. Next to King Tut's tomb, the Ice Man probably had been the most important archaeological discovery of the twentieth century. And she hadn't been a part of it.

She was stuck in Amarillo, Texas, at the local public library where she answered reference questions, helped patrons use the computerized card catalog, and found misplaced microfilm for the genealogy club.

If there was not a mummy to be found in her future any time soon—that is, any time between the present and her eligibility for Medicare—then she would take a skeleton. Skeletons were less close to her heart than mummies, but she would take what she could get. She wasn't getting any younger; in fact, this morning, under the theatrical-strength bathroom lights Megan saw what she believed was a very faint line at the corner of her right eye.

Megan listened to the breeze rustling the leaves of the cottonwood trees that shaded the readers club. It was a beautiful, peaceful sound, but it didn't soothe her. She peeled one leg off the vinyl, then the other, and shifted restlessly in the lawn chair. She knew the source of her restlessness and discontent. She was bored and growing older with each passing day. Life and youth were passing her by. And what had she done in her profession? Nothing. She was in a professional vegetative state. If it weren't for Ryan and the intellectual stimulation of the Murder by the Yard Reading Circle and their weekly discussion of mysteries, she would be forced into some dangerous hobby like skydiving or hang gliding just so she would feel she was alive by risking death. Except Ryan would insist on accompanying her, and he would have some horrible accident that would probably kill him. His parachute wouldn't open, or his hang glider wouldn't glide but plummet to the ground in a cloud of dust and broken bones. For such an athletic man, Dr. Ryan Stevens, Ph.D., widower and her best friend, was the most accident-prone individual she knew. She hoped he could hike up Little Sunday Canyon with her without twisting an ankle.

"Why are you staring at me?" asked Ryan in a whisper.

"Do I have a piece of tomato caught between my teeth?"

Megan said the first thing that occurred to her. "I was admiring your killer blue eyes."

Ryan furtively glanced around the circle, his face red. He always blushed when she complimented his looks, which in her opinion were spectacular: black wavy hair with a sprinkling of silver at the temples, turquoise-blue eyes, fine features, broad shoulders, narrow hips. He was a handsome man, and best of all, he didn't know it. Nothing was more disgusting than a man so vain he gazed in every mirrored surface he passed.

"Would you lower your voice? If Randel Anderson hears you, he'll never let me live it down," whispered Ryan.

"Randel has been delivering a lecture on regional mysteries for the last twenty minutes. He can't hear anything but the sound of his own voice."

"I haven't heard him mention *A Is for Alibi*."

Megan sighed. "Strictly speaking, Sue Grafton is not a regional mystery writer in the sense that we're defining the term. Haven't you read any of the authors we're planning to discuss, Ryan?"

Ryan's face turned even redder. "I picked up a book by that guy Jance at the grocery store. *Rattlesnake Crossing* I think it's called. I haven't gotten around to reading it yet. School just started, and I have to make sure I have my lecture notes in order. You have to stay ahead of college upperclassmen. They've learned just enough to be pains in the butt."

Megan leaned over and patted Ryan's knee. "It's okay. Just stay quiet and maybe no one in Murder by the Yard will notice your not voting on the next author we discuss."

"I'm voting! I'm voting for that Jance guy. I figure since I already have one of his books, I might as well vote for him."

Megan rubbed her temples where a throbbing had begun. "Ryan, didn't you read the cover copy on the back of the book? Didn't you look inside the back cover? Didn't you see J. A. Jance's picture?"

Ryan looked bewildered. Of course, Ryan generally looked bewildered whenever mystery writers were the topic of discussion, because, other than Sue Grafton's *A Is for Alibi,* the only mysteries Megan knew for certain that Ryan had read were the Sherlock Holmes stories and *Murders in the Rue Morgue* by Edgar Allan Poe, both of which he read years ago as a college freshman. Instead, Ryan was an aficionado of Westerns. He had an encyclopedic knowledge of titles, authors, plots, and characters of all the major Western novels and numerous minor ones. He had a collection of first editions by Louis L'Amour with the exception of *Hondo,* which, according to Ryan, is one of L'Amour's finest, and he was in the process of collecting the novels of Les Savage, Jr., whom Ryan claimed was the first and perhaps the best author of psychological Westerns. Megan never asked for a explanation of what constituted a psychological Western. She lacked the necessary background. With the exception of *Shane* she had never read a Western, a fact she had never shared with Ryan.

"J. A. Jance is a woman, Ryan," said Megan, pronouncing each word distinctly.

"Of course she is," said Randel Anderson. "I'm surprised you didn't know that, Ryan." Randel had a supercilious smirk on his face.

So far as Megan was concerned, Randel claimed the prize as the most irritating member of Murder by the Yard ever since he pontificated on Miss Marple's knitting needles as phallic symbols. He was an English teacher at Amarillo College, a local two-year institution, and tended to believe himself an expert on anything literary. He wore a goatee which at least looked less like something one might actually find on a goat since he and Candi Hobbs, another member of the reading circle, had become an item, but Candi hadn't managed to sweeten Randel's disposition to any degree. He had occasionally shown promising signs of a developing sense of humor, so Megan supposed that was a plus. If she lived long enough, she might see a Randel who was socially housebroken. Ryan disagreed. Ryan ground his teeth together every time he and Randel communicated—if you called their bickering communication.

"Megan and I were discussing why J. A. Jance writes under her initials," said Ryan. "It was a private discussion."

Megan noticed his clenched teeth. At least he wasn't grinding his molars.

"Then you should have kept your voice down, old boy." Randel delighted in using English clichés. Megan wouldn't have minded so much if his clichés weren't at least sixty years out of date. She had spent a year in Great Britain as an undergraduate and never heard anyone use the expression "old boy."

Herbert Jackson III, privately nicknamed "Call me Herb" by Megan and Ryan, cleared his throat, a mannerism of his which seemed a necessary precursor to speech. He tugged on a denim vest embroidered with such western symbols as cacti, boots, revolvers, and horses, worn over a denim work shirt and Levis so new they still had a factory crease. Call me Herb was a lawyer and as such was born with an incurable addiction to three-piece suits, no matter what kind. He was writing a legal thriller and insisted on handing out a new chapter each week to the reading circle "for their enjoyment." Neither Megan nor anyone else she knew in the group succeeded in reading more than a page without falling asleep. On a scale of one to ten, Herb's boring factor as a writer was an eleven.

Despite that, Megan liked Call me Herb, three-piece suits and all, since he had defended her more than once when she had gotten involved in murder. Not that she was ever guilty of murder, but she had been a suspect once—well, almost a suspect—she wasn't arrested, but it was a close thing.

"Why does J. A. Jance write under her initials?" asked Herb.

Agnes Caldwell, owner of the Time and Again Bookstore, an establishment that sold both new and used books, where Murder by the Yard usually met when they weren't sharing a picnic lunch in Palo Duro Canyon instead, sat up straight on her camp stool. She was a shriveled gnome of a woman of indeterminate age but probably in her seventies, with silky brown hair twisted into a knot at the back of her head, faded blue eyes under hooded lids, and a tongue like a rapier. She usually kept it sheathed, but could draw it and behead an opponent so expertly that he wouldn't know it until his head toppled off his shoulders. She wore support hose under slacks, sensible shoes with crepe soles, and a sweater all year round. Megan claimed that Agnes reminded her of her great-grandmother Christy, except Megan's granny divorced the last of her five husband at age eighty-seven, and Agnes was a spinster.

"I don't know in Jance's case," said Agnes, "but other women mystery novelists choose to write under their initials to avoid the whole gender issue. I have several male readers who won't knowingly read women writers, and conversely, I have women readers who won't read male writers. Writing under initials sufficiently muddies the water that I can persuade both my male and female readers to do some cross-gender reading without their being aware of it until it's too late. Of course, with the trend of publishers to plaster their authors' pictures somewhere on the book, initials don't fool anyone these days."

"That sounds like cross-dressing," said Randel with a snicker. It was the kind of remark Megan expected from him. Sensitivity and Randel were not acquainted.

Rosemary Pittman gave Randel a disapproving look, then smiled at the rest of the circle. "Prejudice is so senseless. I would certainly hate to do without my Aaron Elkins, John D. McDonald, and Tony Hillerman just because they are male writers."

"I'd miss reading Carolyn Hart and Charlotte MacLeod," said Lieutenant Ray Roberts, sitting between Rosemary and Lorene. The Twins were taken with the retired police lieutenant who had assisted in Megan's last homicide case, and as far as Megan could tell, he enjoyed being fussed over by the two elderly women. "When I was a cop there's no way I would have put up with amateur sleuths, but that was real life. Now that I'm retired I read for fun, not for realism. Professor Shandy cracks me up."

Ryan leaned over to whisper to Megan. "I don't remember any Professor Shandy among the authors we're considering."

Megan patted his hand. "Just lean back and enjoy the canyon and the sunshine and the warm weather, Ryan. Or have another of Lorene's chocolate chip cookies and a glass of tea, but please don't make any comments that anyone else but Agnes and I can hear."

Ryan looked bewildered again. "Agnes?"

"She's the only other person in the reading circle who knows you're a fraud and will keep it a secret."

Ryan's face took on an irritated expression, and Megan knew he hated being reminded that he was masquerading as a mystery reader. Not that he would drop out of the reading circle. The threat of mutilation wouldn't keep him away from the weekly meetings, not as long as she was a member. Ryan believed that if they weren't joined at the hip like Siamese twins, she would act out the part of an amateur sleuth and end up in jail for obstructing justice, if not on some worse charge. As far as he was concerned, he was all that stood between her and legal disaster. He didn't understand that her involvement with murder cases was a matter of coincidence. She didn't deliberately seek out bodies dispatched with violence by their fellow man—or woman—she just happened to be in the right place at the right time to stumble over corpses. It wasn't her fault.

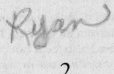

2

PALO DURO CANYON, PRESENT DAY

How was I supposed to know that J. A. Jance is a woman? I just picked up the book at my local grocery store because it was by one of the authors the members of Murder by the Yard were excited about. I didn't look at the book other than the title. *Rattlesnake Crossing* has a certain ring to it. It reminds me of the Texas Panhandle, so I ought to at least like the setting of the book. I ought to feel right at home. We have enough rattlesnakes around here to send a herpetologist into ecstasy. I thought if I got around to reading the book, I might feel an empathy with the main character, whom I notice from reading the front cover is a sheriff, not some amateur sleuth, so I won't have to worry about Megan copying her actions.

Excuse me, but I have let my frustration over being caught with my ignorance showing distract me. My name is Ryan Stevens, and I am curator of history at the Panhandle-Plains Museum on the West Texas A&M University campus, where I also teach two courses in American history: *Manifest Destiny and Westward Expansion in the Nineteenth Century,* and *Frontier Life in the American West.* I also teach a seminar every Monday night which is open to the public: *George Armstrong Custer and the Battle of the Little Big Horn.* I'm flattered that every seat in the auditorium is filled, but it's the subject, not the teacher. If Custer had won at the Little Big Horn, no one would attend my seminar but the graduate students who are forced to. A massacre, like other examples of mass murder, always packs the house.

But enough about Custer. The reader can check out one of the many available biographies if more information on the boy general is needed or wanted. What is more to my purpose is a brief biography of Megan Clark, or Dr. Megan Elizabeth Clark, Ph.D., and a revealing discussion of our relationship. Megan lives next door to me and has all her life except the eight years she was away at school. Her mother lives there, too, but don't think that means that Megan is returning to the womb. Although I'm certain that Megan's mother has a womb, she is not the sort of woman to let it influence her. She is not motherly, as my deceased wife used to say, although I'm sure she loves Megan as much as any woman loves her offspring. Megan and her mother share the white frame house next door as two roommates would. It allows Megan to save money to sponsor a dig and also to pay down her student loans. I'm not certain what benefit Megan's mother derives from the arrangement. Perhaps just intelligent conversation.

To continue, Megan was my oldest daughter's best friend during their growing-up years. Now she is my best friend. I am not a father figure for various reasons—the primary ones

being my ignorance of the internal combustion engine and
my inability to engage in such athletic endeavors as rock
climbing, waterskiing, or canoeing without requiring emergency treatment for minor injuries. I don't know the reason
for this clumsiness of mine. I can walk across a room without falling over the coffee table or knocking over a lamp. I
am in good physical condition—much better, in fact, that
many men half my age—but I always injure myself whenever I accompany Megan on one of her sporting activities.
Just for the record, I do not consider rock climbing to be a
safe activity, and my opinion is not influenced by my sus-
taining a broken wrist while climbing up a cliff in Palo Duro
Canyon with Megan. Of course, I am not an aficionado of
any sort of climbing, be it trees, mountains, or ladders, since
I keep my distance from any activity which results in my being more than two feet above the ground. I have a phobia.
I'm not ashamed of it, but I don't mention it to Megan either
for an excellent reason. I'm in love with her, but I'm also
nineteen years older. I mention nothing about myself that
might put me at a disadvantage when compared to a younger
man—particularly when that younger man is Jerry Carr.

You haven't been introduced to Jerry Carr yet, so I will
provide a thumbnail biography. He is the lieutenant in
charge of the Special Crimes Unit which investigates suspicious death in Potter, Randall, or Armstrong counties of
the Texas Panhandle. He once dated Megan, but she put the
relationship on hold after he suspected her of murder. He
had good reason, mind you, but the evidence was planted in
order to frame Megan, and she felt he ought to have known
it. I thought so, too. At any rate, Megan has not kept company with Jerry Carr since, and I'll do my best to interfere
if he tries to insinuate himself back into her good graces.
All right, so I'm jealous. I'll admit it. I'm a pitiful case—a
clumsy professor in his mid-forties in love with a cute

young woman. I've never told her and probably never will.

Did I mention Megan was cute? It is not a word I say out loud when I'm around her, because she reacts strongly to the "C word" as she calls it. Nevertheless, she's cute. She is five feet, two inches if she stretches or wears thick soles, has curly red hair and a smattering of freckles across her nose, and her eyes are the color of fine bourbon. She is small and lithe, has a square jaw and a pointed chin, and is stubborn as a Missouri mule. I don't mention her stubbornness any more than I refer to her as "cute" within her hearing. Megan can react in a volatile manner.

So what does Megan get out of our relationship? Not sex. I haven't the courage to make a sexual overture, not for fear of being turned down with a kindly pat on the cheek, although that would hurt, but because I'm afraid she would be so horrified by such behavior than she would terminate our relationship.

On the other hand, maybe she wouldn't.

But I'm afraid to test the bounds of what we share, so we'll continue on as we are.

And who are we? We are Holmes and Watson. Let me be more specific. For the past six months or more I have been Watson to Megan's Sherlock Holmes while she has played amateur sleuth in three different investigations. I have been her Watson because I have been writing down these adventures—if you want to call them that—but mostly I have been trying to protect her from her own worst instincts. She persists in getting involved in murder investigations and putting herself at risk. It has only been through the grace of God and good luck that she has not been a victim of one of the murderers she has pursued. Actually, in one instance it was not God or good luck that saved her: it was a used dictionary, but that is another story. To continue with this one. How does a white, middle-class young woman, the least likely category of person to be involved in murder, manage to discover murder victims not once, not twice, but three times? Let me correct myself. Three is the number of cases we—she—has been involved in. The body count is actually higher than three. How is this possible? Statistically, it isn't. It defies logic that the same white, middle-class young woman could continue to discover dead bodies. But it happens, and as long as it does, I'll be by her side, protecting her from herself.

Why, you ask, am I Watson? As the older, or rather, more mature of the partners, why don't I play the lead role of Holmes? Very simple. I don't do bodies. I particularly don't do bodies that are seeping. I hold the Amarillo record for the longest sustained fainting spell on the occasion of Megan's first discovery of a dead body. I faint at the sight of blood. Even thinking about it makes me lightheaded. It is impossible to investigate a crime scene—as Megan always does before Special Crimes arrives—while one is unconscious.

So I am Watson and she is Holmes. She's better in that role.

But that doesn't mean I plan to let her become involved in murder again, and I am safe in saying that, since I doubt we'll stumble across a body while on a picnic in Palo Duro Canyon.

3

PALO DURO CANYON, 1868

Spotted Tongue ran down the canyon toward the horse herd, hearing the sounds of the camp fall silent as the children and the other women stop to stare after him. Most of the men who had gone on the raid, probably the last one before it was time to hunt buffalo so that the women might dry meat for the winter, were still sleeping off the effects of last night's celebration. The warriors had returned with many horses, several captives, and much food. The two male captives were given to the women for sport; the three female captives were claimed by their captors as slaves. Little Flower had cowered in the arbor and covered her ears. Spotted Tongue followed as he always did after a raid. He did not take her but only held her in his arms. Sometimes he would put his hand over her mouth, so the People would not hear the sounds she made and know that she was rejecting their ways. He did not speak her tongue but he did not need to. He recognized curses when he heard them in whatever tongue, and so would the rest of the Nermernuh. Last night as he held her, he only hoped she did not bring bad medicine to the People.

The captives' screams had finally ceased near dawn and Little Flower's rigid body relaxed in his arms, her voice, now reduced to hoarse whispers, fell silent, and she slept. Her eyes were swollen and red from tears and lack of sleep when Green Willow woke her to go pick the wild plums. Spotted Tongue had left her to drag the captives' bodies away from the camp, so Little Flower would not see them. He had felt Green Willow watching him from her arbor and wondered what she was thinking. He grew curious about what women thought only after he captured Little Flower and made her his second wife. Before that he didn't care.

Spotted Tongue's thoughts were fierce and his belly began to hurt again. Little Flower was not reconciled to her place and carried sorrow about with her despite all he could do. She must know that he will not return her to her people, especially not now. She must make her home with the Nermernuh—those the white man called the Comanche. She must become one of them. He could not protect her from the other women if she held herself apart from him. Already she had been beaten for running away. He felt dirty afterwards and vowed he would not beat her again. But why must she keep trying to leave the Nermernuh? She belonged to him, and he tried to understand her ways. But her people were not the most human of men. She must understand that the Nermernuh were. She must adapt, she must learn. Even now, five full moons after her capture, she refused to learn to speak his language. She knew not one word. He told her in sign language the way she must behave, the proper way of a way of a woman of the Nermernuh. But Little Flower stared at him with wide-open *eyes, confused, sorrowful, without understanding. Or did she understand? Sometimes he thought she did. Sometimes he caught a glimpse of knowing, almost of being, as though she knew who she was and was determined not to give herself up to the ways of the Nermernuh. He did not like that, but he treated her gently anyway. Sometimes she cried when he was gentle with her, but silently as he had taught her, the tears spilling out of her eyes and coursing down her cheeks without a sound from her. A crying woman or a crying baby endangered the People. Their enemies might hear and attack them. Only on the prairie deep inside the land where the Nermernuh roamed; or in the canyon that protected them when the snows came, was it safe to make sound without fear, to sing of victory, to mourn the fallen warrior.*

He wondered if Little Flower would mourn him if he fell to the guns of the white soldiers or the Tejanos. He thought not.

Even though he, Spotted Tongue, was all who stood between her and those who desired her or who wished her dead because she was one of an inferior race, she held herself apart from him. She captured his spirit as surely as he captured the white mare. How could she hold such power over him? Like good luck came without making medicine? Did the spirit of the most feared Cannibal Owl dwell within her? Was that the reason his medicine had left him? But no; he lost his ability to make medicine before he captured her, not after.

Sometimes he watched her in the flickering light of the fire, and felt his spirit swell inside his chest. Her beauty pierced his heart like a lance. Little Flower was like a doe with a very delicate body, soft and warm to touch—but tall, nearly as tall as he, and he was the tallest in the band. She was so different, yet still a woman, still his woman.

He caught his pony, half-hitching the war bridle made of horse hair about its jaw. He kicked his horse with his moccasin-clad feet, these moccasins made by Little Flower. The beaded pattern was different from that of other men's moccasins. Perhaps that was how he felt the power of her spirit; perhaps that was why his thoughts were new and different from other warriors. Perhaps her medicine was in the moccasins. But he would not kick them off. He hunted well while wearing them. He had fought well, too, slaying a family of Tejanos on the last raid he led. The Tejanos were his blood enemies, and the children of this family were too old to adopt. They would not accept the customs of the Nermernuh, so he slew them. Little Flower saw the bloody scalps hanging from his lance, but said nothing just as he had hoped. The dead were not of her clan.

He did not know why she cried in his arms that night.

Spotted Tongue rode his pony down the small, side canyon, its walls shorter and not nearly so steep as the main one where the Nermernuh built their arbors. The plum thickets grew along the bottom where in spring, when it rained, a narrow, shallow stream watered their roots. He slid off his horse and silently hunted the tracks of his women, Green Willow, and the other one, Little Flower, the precious one he would not lose. The stream was dry and had been for the passing of several moons, but those who walked on its sandy banks left faint tracks. He slid from his pony's back and crouched to study the barely visible moccasin prints. He recognized Little Flower's long and narrow footprints among the broader ones of the other women. He must follow her tracks before the sun set.

He saw a scuffed place on the sandy bank and marks of a body being dragged away. He followed the drag marks, his heart pounding inside his chest again, and fear taking *the place of his worry. When he found Little Flower around a curve of the path near the big rock, her spirit had already fled her body. His scream echoed from the canyon walls as he fell to his knees and cradled her body in his arms. As he stroked her long black hair, he felt a soft place the size of his palm in the back of Little Flower's head. He looked around and saw a large smooth rock with her blood not quite dry on its surface. Someone had tried to hide the bloody stone among the wild red plums.*

Murder had been done.

Spotted Tongue rode back to his arbor and slid off his horse, feeding his spirit on rage and grief. He must dress Little Flower for her burial. He would not allow the women to do it even if any of them volunteered. Warriors did not dress the dead and prepare them for what lay beyond the sun, but what was one more step away from the way of the People? He already walked alone in the wilderness.

Spotted Tongue ducked under the brush arbor he had shared with Little Flower, glad that Green Willow was in her own arbor, so he did not have to talk to her. He found Little Flower's buffalo-skin case that held a dress of soft white buckskin with wide fringe at the hem and the sleeves. He remembered how long she worked because she wanted her dress that white color instead of the yellow of most dresses the other women wore. She had decorated the dress with red beads and silver conchos he had bought for her from the Comancheros. Her moccasins also had red beads on them. She had never worn the dress or moccasins. He didn't know why she made them unless her spirit told her she would die in this canyon, and she wanted beautiful clothes for her trip beyond the sun, where there were buffalo as numerous as blades of grass, and the Nermernuh never again would know hunger or sickness or sorrow. Surely he would join her. Surely whatever Great Spirit she believed in would not separate them after death.

He felt the touch of Green Willow's bitter eyes as she watched him. He looked at her sitting in her arbor, and his fury nearly overcame him. Of all the Nermernuh only Green Willow hated Little Flower for who she was: his second wife whom he loved more than his life, maybe even more than the Nermernuh. Everyone else hated her for what she was: a foreigner, not of the People. Even though Little Flower was his second wife, and thus adopted into the tribe and had become a Nerm, a Human Being, too many hated her for her pride. She would not accept that she was second wife and thus must be obedient and humble. Little Flower possessed the pride of a warrior. She lowered her eyes for no woman—or man. She was too proud to kneel to the superiority of the Nermernuh. He froze as the thought struck him that what was surprising was not that Little Flower was murdered, but that she avoided murder for so long.

Spotted Tongue watched Green Willow leave her arbor and walk by herself out of the camp. It would do her no good to walk away to wait for his anger to pass. He would hold his anger in his heart until he found Little Flower's murderer. So intent was he in staring at Green Willow that he allowed a warrior to walk up to his arbor without hearing him.

"What are you doing with that dress? You going to start wearing dresses and cooking for us? If you're going to live like a woman, can I buy Little Flower? You won't be any good for her; she needs what a real man can give her. What's

your answer, Spotted Tongue? I'll give you a hundred horses for her."

Spotted Tongue recognized the voice and turned around slowly. He had found a target for his rage—or the target had found him. "Coyote Dung! I thought I smelled something, but I hoped I was wrong. Since I am not, why don't you stand over by the creek? I have to sleep in this arbor tonight and I do not want you stinking it up. By the way, did the Tejanos smell you when you led the raid? Is that how they found you? I heard you lost half the horses you stole trying to escape."

"Where did you hear that?" asked the warrior, scowling at Spotted Tongue.

Coyote Dung was a short, squat man whose bulky shoulders, bandy legs, and massive head with heavy features made him look like he was molded by a young child playing with mud. He was man shape, but that was the most complimentary thing Spotted Tongue could say. He had a temper that exploded like a bullet from a white man's gun. As a ferocious warrior and one of the best horseman among the Kwahadi, the band of Nermernuh to which they both belonged, Coyote Dung earned the warriors' respect to temper the revulsion his appearance caused. Spotted Tongue's friend, Fat Belly, always said that Coyote Dung's looks would make a vulture throw up, but even a vulture would go behind a bush where Coyote Dung couldn't see him do it.

"And you smell like an Apache! Did your mother let an Apache captive crawl into her tipi?" Spotted Tongue's final question changed Coyote Dung's scowl into a teeth-bearing snarl. There were worse insults, but being accused of being the get of an Apache was bad enough. The Apaches were a filthy tribe.

Raging like a bull buffalo, spitting out insults against

Spotted Tongue's ancestors back to the mating of the animals that brought forth the People, and moving quicker than a striking snake, Coyote Dung grabbed him in an embrace that Spotted Tongue knew would crush his chest. He would spit up blood until he died—which might take several hours. He could not die; he could not leave Little Flower's burial to the mercy of others.

While Spotted Tongue's arms were captured in Coyote Dung's crushing embrace, he could move one hand enough to reach out and draw the ugly warrior's knife. He sank it a finger's width into the flesh just above Coyote Dung's groin. "Let me go—or I will push this knife up to the hilt in your belly!"

"You're a piece of rotting buffalo meat that I wouldn't throw to my dogs!" said Coyote Dung, trying to push away the hand holding the knife.

With an effort Spotted Tongue pushed the knife deeper. "Let me go before we kill one another, Coyote Dung. There would be no honor in either death."

Panting, Coyote Dung let Spotted Tongue loose and pushed him away. "We'll fight again, and next time I'll bring my knife."

He stalked away, and Spotted Tongue dropped onto his blanket, glad that Coyote Dung hadn't noticed that he had stolen the warrior's knife. He didn't want to fight Coyote Dung for a while. He took several deep breaths, each one hurting like knife cuts across his chest. Gradually, his heart and breathing slowed. "That was really smart, Spotted Tongue," he said aloud. "You aren't satisfied with outdoing Coyote Dung, you have to give him an excuse to throw you off the cliff." He remembered Little Flower's limp body lying in the dirt waiting for burial and decided he didn't care if Coyote Dung killed him the next time or not. With the loss of his medicine and the death of Little Flower, what life was left to him stretched out like an endless blizzard that wiped away warmth and pleasure and sent cold and sorrow instead?

"I wouldn't worry about the cliff, Spotted Tongue, but next war party or raid, I wouldn't ride in front of Coyote Dung if I were you."

Spotted Tongue struggled to his feet, feeling that knife-like pain in his chest again. "You're right, Fat Belly. You have always told me not to push Coyote Dung, that he would make a bad enemy, but I am a bad enemy, too. And I'm smarter than he is."

Fat Belly was tall with a paunch that hung over his breechclout and a face whose broad features mirrored his good nature. "But you wouldn't shoot him in the back during a battle. I wouldn't put that past Coyote Dung. He's brother to the weasel."

Spotted Tongue leaned over to pick up Little Flower's dress and moccasins off the ground. He grabbed his side so he could straighten up. "I would sooner trust a weasel."

Fat Belly helped him up. "How bad did Coyote Dung hurt you? Do you want me to get Otter Belt?"

Spotted Tongue shook his head as he stepped away from his friend. "I wouldn't trust that old man to remove a cactus thorn. Why would I trust him to fix my ribs?"

"What's wrong with your ribs?"

Fat Belly was good natured, but sometimes he was slow to understand. "That son of a Tonkawa whore broke some of my ribs," said Spotted Tongue, folding up Little Flower's dress to make a less noticeable bundle. Not that he cared if the other warriors made fun of him, but he didn't want to talk about Little Flower, and he certainly didn't want anyone either watching or helping him bury her.

"Uh, Spotted Tongue, what are you doing with Little Flower's dress?"

Spotted Tongue looked at Fat Belly's worried face and swallowed hard to keep from crying. Warriors did not cry. "Little Flower is dead—murdered, and I go to bury her."

Sorrow immediately appeared in Fat Belly's eyes and he put his hand on Spotted Tongue's shoulder in a gesture of comfort. "In the name of the spirit of the wolf, who killed her? Where?"

Spotted Tongue looked into the distance without seeing the cliffs towering over the canyon floor. "I don't know who, but I will find out. When I do, I will hunt down and kill whoever it is. It's my right because she was my wife." He ducked out of the brush arbor followed by Fat Belly. "As to where she was murdered, in that small canyon across the stream. Stand at its mouth, Fat Belly, and keep everyone away. No one liked her when she was alive. I won't have anyone watching while I bury her. At least the murderer didn't mutilate her body so she couldn't travel beyond the sun."

"I liked her," said Fat Belly as Spotted Tongue mounted his pony.

Spotted Tongue gathered up the horse-hair rope knotted around his pony's lower jaw and looked down at his friend. "Then do this last thing for her, Fat Belly. You know she would hate anyone staring at her, and I'll be watching over her burial place tonight. I want to be alone with her one last time to—to say good-bye."

Fat Belly nodded and slapped the pony's rump, startling it into a gallop. "May the spirit of the wolf go with you."

Spotted Tongue's pony jumped the narrow stream and galloped up the small canyon. As the body of Little Flower came into view Spotted Tongue pulled up his pony and slid off its back. With no one to hear him he allowed himself to

groan with the pain riding his pony caused. He straightened as much as he was able, tied his pony's rope to a salt
cedar bush, and knelt down by his beloved second wife's
body. "I'm back, Little Flower. I brought your new dress.
I'm sorry you never wore it for me. Until now."

Feverishly he stripped off her old dress as he talked to
her as if she could hear him. His throat hurt from trying to
suppress his tears until he decided she might like it if he
cried. His voice sounded thick to his own ears, but her
spirit would understand him. That she didn't speak his
tongue in life meant nothing. Spirits of the dead understood all tongues.

He pulled on her new dress, slipped on her moccasins,
and smoothed her hair. "I loved you, Little Flower. With you
in my tipi I was happy. Even the pain in my head from wondering why I couldn't make medicine was better when I
could look up and see you roasting buffalo meat for me.
Colors were brighter, the wind sang with a hundred voices
through the cottonwood trees when you stood beneath them.
I'm a warrior and sometimes a war chief, I cannot think of
the words I need to say to tell you how I feel. I hope your
spirit can hear what my heart says."

Unable to speak again, in silence, he dug a grave with
his knife in the shadow of a huge stone as high as his head.
Then he used the same knife to cut off his braids below his
ears. To men of the People, hair was almost sacred, and
there could be no greater gesture of sorrow he could make
than to fold her hands over her chest, and lace his braids
between her fingers.

Spotted Tongue picked Little Flower up and laid her in
her grave, ignoring the pain that knifed through his chest.
He covered her face and body with a blanket because he
could not stand to throw dirt on her. The last thing he did

for her was to roll the huge rock on the grave. Then he threw himself face down on the ground to mourn. No one saw him but a wolf who watched over him until dawn when it quietly padded away.

20 minutes

not Ryan

2 pgs

4

The world's nothing but a graveyard filled with old bones.

—Julian Christenberry, medieval
weaponry expert, to Philip St. Ives in
Oliver Bleeck's *The Highbinders*, 1974

PALO DURO CANYON, PRESENT DAY

Megan peeled herself out of the lawn chair and rubbed the backs of her bare thighs where there was now a set pattern of woven plastic strips. Be damned if she would sit in that chair again. When everybody came back from their walk up Little Sunday Canyon, she was going to sit on Call me Herb's blanket with him. Ryan could whistle up the wind if he didn't like it—and he wouldn't like it. He thought she ought to sit by him. One would think that he was afraid that Randal or Call me Herb or both were after her chastity. But then he has been in a bad mood all day, starting at lunch when he complained about the sandwiches she made. . . .

"Megan, there's a hair on my sandwich," said Ryan, peering at the top slice of bread on his pickle and pimento-loaf sandwich. "It's a black hair. Who in your house has black hair?"

Megan reached over and picked up the hair. "It belongs

to either Rembrandt or Horatio. Next time I'll be sure to tell them to shed only their white hair on your white bread. Then you won't notice it."

Ryan stared at her with a horrified look on his face. "It's a *dog* hair!"

Megan shrugged her shoulders. "Think of it as a condiment."

"My God, Megan!"

Megan took the sandwich out of Ryan's hands. "If you're going to be so touchy about a little dog hair, I'll get you another sandwich, and I'll eat this one."

Ryan looked at the picnic basket. "What other kind of sandwiches did you pack?"

"Peanut butter and jelly."

"Peanut butter and jelly?" He shook his head. "Never mind. I'll fill up on potato chips and cookies with a beer chaser. Can you get me one out of the cooler while you're up?"

Still smarting from his complaint about dog hair—he acted like she was trying to poison him—Megan started to tell him to get it himself, then relented. He was always so good about going with her whenever she went hiking or rock climbing or rowing even when he was allergic to everything that blew and grew and had no interest in her outdoor hobbies. But he went anyway just to keep her company and never once complained even when his hiking boots rubbed such blisters on his feet that he had to walk the three miles back to her pickup in his socks. She never knew that blisters could bleed so much. She'd had to blindfold him and lead him by the hand so he wouldn't accidentally see his blood soaking through the heels and toes of his socks. Ryan fainted at the sight of someone else's blood. The Lord only knew what he would do at the sight of his own. Probably go into a coma. . . .

Megan smiled at the memory of that hike. He had looked so gorgeous that day in his tight Levis and work shirt. A real hunk. She wondered why he didn't date.

"Why are you staring at me with that grin on your face? Are you plotting some prank to get back at me for making such an ass out of myself over the dog hair." He glanced at Megan's two beagles whose long leashes were tied to a tree branch. "Rembrandt looks like he's lost some weight. He doesn't look so much like a beer keg on legs."

She felt her throat begin to tighten. She had managed not to think about the truth all day—until now. She struggled to prevent her voice from wobbling when she spoke. "That's because he's dying, Ryan. He has cancer of the mouth and throat and there's nothing the vet can do. I brought him and Horatio with us today so Rembrandt could hike in the canyon one last time. When the cancer gets to the point that he can't eat or drink, I'll have the vet put him to sleep. But it'll be so hard to let him go." Her chin quivered and she tightened her lip in an effort not to cry.

Ryan stood up and gathered her in his arms. He pressed her head against his chest when he heard a quiet sob. "I'm so sorry, honey," he said, whispering the words into her red hair.

"Hey, none of that, you two!" said Randel. "It's broad daylight, and you're embarrassing us."

"Shut up, Randel. We couldn't embarrass you if we stole your clothes and you had to walk home with your bare behind hanging out. Besides, it's not what you think," said Ryan.

Randel sniggered. "You could have fooled me, old boy."

"That wouldn't be hard to do," said Agnes, pushing herself out of another lawn chair and walking over to Ryan and Megan. She tucked Megan's hair behind her ears. "The minute I saw your shoulders heaving I knew you were crying. What's wrong, sweetie? Did you pinch yourself on that old lawn chair, or are you not feeling well? Do you need to go home?"

Megan twisted out of Ryan's arms and got a paper napkin out of the picnic basket. She wiped her eyes and blew her nose. "I'm fine, Agnes. Don't baby me. I just need to walk the dogs, let them find a proper tree to water. Believe me, you don't want them taking care of nature too close to our picnic area, not if we have to sit here for our discussion time." She sniffed once, blew her nose again, and tossed the napkin in the waste-disposal barrel. "Come on, boys, let's take a walk," she said, untying the dogs' leashes from the tree limb.

Ryan started to follow, but Agnes grasped his arm. "What's wrong with Megan?"

Megan heard Agnes whispering to Ryan and Ryan whispering back. The acoustics in the canyon were incredible. She could hear almost everything they said. She knew that Agnes would pass the word along to everybody, and she hoped no one would offer her sympathy. The hurt was too close to her heart to talk about.

The variegated canyon walls of orange and red and brown rose a hundred feet straight up from the dry, narrow creek bed, choked with plum thickets, sage, and cedar. Half-buried in the sandy soil less that fifty feet up the west canyon wall was the room-sized, golden sandstone rock called Indian Rock because one could easily imagine a Comanche brave standing motionless peering down the length of Palo Duro Canyon, watching for the only predator which threatened the People: the white man.

Megan glanced up at Indian Rock and tightened her hold on her beagles' leashes before trudging up the side of the canyon toward it. Rembrandt and Horatio shamelessly begged for food at the picnic, and it didn't help that every

single member of Murder by the Yard Reading Circle
fed them bits and pieces of hot dogs, hamburgers, baked
beans, and cookies. Horatio's stomach was so full it looked
like he had swallowed a volleyball. Rembrandt had hardly
been able to eat anything at all. It broke her heart watching
him try.

She walked along the sandy path that paralleled the dry
stream bed, matching her speed to Rembrandt's pace so he
wouldn't wear himself out trying to keep up. Horatio occasionally pulled on his leash hard enough to choke himself
as he darted from side to side of the path investigating all
the interesting smells, and to a beagle everything smelled
interesting. "Slow down, Horatio, you're sniffing so hard
you'll hyperventilate."

He didn't listen, of course, just looked back at her as if
to say, "Did you say something, Big Person Who Sleeps
With Me?" Horatio most often obeyed if there was something in it for him.

She loosened his leash a little and walked on. She wondered how old the path was. It was a good five inches lower
than the surrounding ground. So many feet had walked this
way over time. Perhaps the Comanche women had walked
along this same path. There were wild plum thickets all
along this offshoot canyon—in fact, they lined one side
of the path—and Megan knew the women would gather the
plums along with mustang grapes. Along the riverbanks farther east off the caprock they would pick pecans, walnuts,
haws, and persimmons. The women would crush these fruits
and nuts, add strips of raw bison meat, crush the mixture together, and dry the meat strips, now flavored with the nuts
and berries, to make pemmican. Despite growing up in the
Texas Panhandle, Megan's knowledge of the Comanche was
hit or miss. She knew about pemmican because local companies made and sold meat strips they called pemmican.

Which it wasn't really, but it was hard to get ahold of real bison meat. She made a mental note to herself to check out a few books on the Comanche from the library. It was almost sinful for an anthropologist, which she technically was, to know so little about the Amerindians, particularly the Kwahadi band of the Comanche, those whose stomping grounds, so to speak, was the Palo Duro Canyon.

Megan held tightly to her dogs' leashes. If she dropped the leashes or they slipped through her fingers, Rembrandt and Horatio would disappear so fast she wouldn't see them for their dust. Well, maybe not Rembrandt. He was seventeen years old and very sick. He could hardly get up off his pillow and walk. She had to lift him up on the bed at night because he could no longer jump, and he didn't sleep well anywhere but at the foot of her bed. Horatio curled up on her pillow after she fell asleep. She would wake up in the middle of the night to the sound of his snoring in her ear. As the son of a rancher, Ryan had a practical view of animals and he didn't believe any animal, be it cat, dog, bird, lizard, whatever had fur, feathers, or scales, belonged in the house. He had learned not to say anything about it anymore in her presence.

Megan felt the sun beating down on her face and her shoulders where her tank top left them bare. She hoped she had enough sunscreen on. She hated it when she sunburned, not only because it was painful, but also because she freckled. Bad enough to be very short with red curly hair that everyone wanted to touch, without the further embarrassment of freckles. Complete strangers would walk up to her in a store to tell her how cute her freckles were. Megan noticed it was always the people without freckles who thought they were so damn cute. Somebody ought to invent a foolproof freckle bleach. He would make a fortune. She didn't know how the inventor could test the preparation, though. She couldn't think of any other animal except humans who had freckles. Oh, well, another brilliant idea proved totally impractical.

Megan wished she could hear the cicadas singing, or the rustling of little animals in the underbrush, but with the dogs along, all the little animals, including the cicadas, were hiding in their burrows, or wherever they lived. She and Ryan would have to drive the eighteen miles to Palo Duro again tomorrow to sit on Indian Rock and listen to the all the myriad sounds of mammals and lizards and insects.

She wrapped the leashes around one hand and wiped the sweat off her forehead with the hem of her tank top. It was hot for a September afternoon, and the air was still. Not a leaf moved on the plum bushes, which was odd. Not a hundred feet away she had listened to the wind rustle through the cottonwood leaves, yet now it was abnormally still. It must be because she was walking up this small canyon, and its walls cut off the movement of air. It was not only still, but quiet, too. Abnormally quiet, even considering that the presence of the dogs frightened the other animals. She swallowed, feeling as if she was caught in a stop-action film. She laughed at herself. She had always had a vivid imagination. She even imagined she could hear the hoof beats of the huge Comanche pony herd which had grazed farther south in the canyon when the People wintered in the Palo Duro. In fact, she heard hoof beats behind her, faint but distinct, and caught a faint sour odor of human sweat. She felt a chill raise goose bumps on her arms and whirled around to look behind her. Nothing. The path was empty. Her heart pounded in her chest. If she closed her eyes and listened hard, she could imagine hearing the guttural sounds of Comanche speech, the laughter of children, the barking of dogs.

She opened her eyes. Actually, she did hear the barking

of dogs. Rembrandt and Horatio pulled against their leashes and bayed frantically at Indian Rock. Megan noticed that the huge stone appeared to have rolled a few feet farther down the side of the canyon at the same time that Rembrandt demonstrated that he still had life in him by jerking his leash out of her hand and running—well, waddling rapidly—toward the giant rock. In her fear that Rembrandt would run away and get lost, she didn't keep a strong grip on Horatio's leash, and the younger, stronger beagle took after his pack mate, his deep, loud baying echoing off the canyon walls. Horatio overtook Rembrandt and passed him like he was driving a hot car at a NASCAR race. Megan made a dive for Rembrandt's leash since he was moving about fast as a tortoise with sore feet. She missed and did a belly flop on the sandy path.

Megan rose up on her knees, her chest and bare legs coated with the fine sand, thanks to the sticky sunscreen. "Rembrandt! Horatio!" she yelled. "You damn dogs, don't you dare run off! I'll send you to the garage without any dog chow! As soon as I catch you two, I'll skin you both alive and make myself a tri-color vest." Tears rolled down her cheeks. "Rembrandt! You're supposed to be sick, damn it, and look at you! Chasing rabbits or squirrels or whatever isn't good for you."

Two strong hands circled her waist and lifted her to her feet. "Don't panic, honey. I'll help catch the dogs."

Megan started running up the path. "Ryan, stay behind me and get ready to catch Horatio if I miss him! Damn you, Horatio, come here!"

"I'll take the dry stream bed, Megan," called Herb, hurrying after Ryan. "If he comes down this way, I'll catch him."

Megan followed the path around a gentle curve out of sight of Ryan and Herb. She stopped to gaze in shock at her dogs.

Ryan barreled into Megan's back. He grabbed for her, but she staggered away toward Indian Rock. "I'm sorry, Megan, but I couldn't stop. Did I hurt you?"

She finally caught her balance and ran toward the base of the huge piece of sandstone that was Indian Rock, where the two dogs were busily tugging on a blue cloth of some kind. It was probably some hiker's jacket or sleeping bag the dogs were tearing up and she'd have to pay for it. Horatio won the tug of war, and settled down to shred what Megan now saw was a shirt. Then she froze where she stood, staring at the object beside Horatio. "Oh, my God!"

She fell to her knees with a curse. "Damnation, Horatio, give me that shirt!" she said between clenched teeth as she tried to pry his jaws open, hoping he wouldn't bite her. Horatio growled and Megan recited a litany of imaginative curses that she hadn't used in a long time. Whether Megan shocked Horatio with her curses, or her tone of voice alerted him that she might lock him out of her bedroom, the beagle gave up the shirt, albeit with a growl which she ignored. Horatio's growl was a wimpy one and no good for threatening anything larger than a mouse.

After losing the tug of war, Rembrandt had picked up a bone, carried it a few feet beyond the rock, and laid down, guarding it more closely than the army guarded Fort Knox. "What kind of bone did Rembrandt find?" she heard Ryan ask as he trotted up the last few feet toward her.

"I didn't get a real close look, but I think it was an ulna. Take it away from him, will you, while I tie Horatio to the cedar up there," she said, pointing at a stunted juniper some distance from Indian Rock. "I can't let the dogs make anymore of a mess."

"Did you say 'ulna?'"

She was kneeling on the ground looking at the beagles' discovery. She heard the nervous uncertainty in Ryan's voice and hoped he wasn't going to be difficult about this. "Yes, I said ulna. You know, the long bone of the human arm."

Ryan finally reached her and looked over her shoulder at what she was studying so closely. She felt his body's heat on her back and heard him suck in a breath.

"Oh my God!"

She glanced up to see his eyes roll up in their sockets. She watched as he crumbled to the ground in the most graceful swoon Megan had ever seen. Sighing, she rose, and gingerly stepped over Ryan's body. She'd have to ask Randel and Herb to carry him down to the picnic area where he would be out of the way.

She walked down the slope toward her other beagle. "I suppose that I'll have to rescue that ulna from Rembrandt myself. We won't have a complete skeleton without it."

5

If you're paid well enough for lifting a rock you don't get too queasy at the sight of whatever is crawling underneath it.

—Stanley Ellin's *The Eighth Circle,* 1958

PALO DURO CANYON, PRESENT DAY

I awoke from my faint to find myself lying on Call me Herb's blanket in the middle of the grove of cottonwood trees where we ate our picnic lunch. That was a conclusion reached after analyzing the evidence: the blanket, the cottonwood trees, the cooler full of beer. I heard vehicles driving by on the narrow, two-lane, asphalt road that ran down the length of the public park, and sat up in time to see a big white van drive by, followed by a car belonging to the Randall County Sheriff's Department. It was followed by a white car, a Chevy, I think, with letters on the side of the door announcing the Randall County Justice of the Peace, Precinct Something or the other. I missed reading the precinct number, but it doesn't make any difference. The justices of the peace all do the same thing in Texas when it comes to a body. They view the body, or skeleton in this case, pronounce the victim dead, and examine the evidence and the circumstances at the scene. They order an autopsy, and by studying the evidence, circumstances, and autopsy protocol, determine whether the death is an accident, suicide, natural causes, or homicide. Believe it or not, the JP is legally in charge of the evidence and can confiscate it if he wants until he determines the cause of death and signs the death certificate. Megan tells me that a Texas justice of the peace is an incredibly powerful elected official when a suspicious death, which is any death not occurring under a doctor's care, is reported, if the JP chooses to use his authority. These days when what Megan calls a clean chain of custody of the evidence is so important, most of them are satisfied to pronounce the victim dead, order an autopsy, and leave the evidence to the crime scene technicians. I don't know what the JP will do with a skeleton. Ask the pathologist to count the bones and hope to find the dental records, I guess. But there is one certain fact of which everyone, including myself, will agree: This must be a homicide, because a dead person doesn't bury himself. Someone else has to do that.

I got a beer out of Megan's cooler—after my experience I needed one—and ambled slowly up the path to join the crowd around Indian Rock. If I ambled slowly enough I might not arrive until the skeleton was unearthed and put in its body bag—or whatever skeletons are commonly tucked into. All the way I lectured myself: do not faint, do not faint, do not faint. I would not have fainted in the first place if I had been prepared to see a skeleton. But to look over Megan's shoulder into empty eye sockets and grinning teeth, not to mention that only the skull and torso with arms—minus the ulna—were visible. The rest of the skeleton was still buried, so it looked at first glance as if it was crawling out of its grave. I know that sounds as if I had been watching too many horror movies, but in the first place, the sun was in my eyes, so objects were indistinct, and in the second place, when you're not expecting to see a skeleton, and a skeleton that looked as if it was posing and smiling at you—well, I'm not ashamed of fainting. Frankly, I thought it was a sensible move to make. Let your subconscious reassure you that monsters are not abroad.

I reached Indian Rock just in time for the action. Megan was arguing with Lieutenant Jerry Carr, the head of the Special Crimes Unit. A cold spot formed in my stomach that had nothing to do with the cold beer I was drinking. I pushed between Randel and Agnes to reach the front of the crowd. "Excuse me, I have to hear this."

"Don't mind me, old boy," said Randel. "That rib you cracked with your elbow will heal." There are those who have the gift for delivering sarcastic comments; then there is Randel.

"Give it a rest, Randel," I said, finally reaching Megan. "Megan, I appreciate your calling to report the skeleton, but now that you have, you and your friends can leave. The JP needs to examine the skeleton and advise us what to do. Then the evidence techs need to work the scene." Jerry Carr stood with his arms crossed after wasting his breath, because I could guarantee that Megan had no intention of leaving.

Megan was kneeling by the skeleton. Ray Roberts, a retired lieutenant of the Amarillo Police Department stood by her, holding what looked like a tackle box—except it wasn't. It was Megan's dig kit which she takes along whenever she goes on a dig. It contains a digital camera, several artists' brushes of varying sizes, a dental pick, a caliper, a small drawing pad, graph paper, garden trowel, a large tea strainer, and I don't know what else, the kitchen sink maybe. She keeps the kit in her behemoth of a GMC pickup with its extended cab, manual shift, and 200,000 miles on the odometer the last time I looked. If Megan had her dig kit, she was getting ready to interfere in another police investigation.

I leaned over and rested my hands on her shoulders. "Come on, Megan, let's go back to the picnic area and everybody have a soft drink. We don't want to get in the lieutenant's way. Besides, we need to discuss this week's book." Megan ignored me totally. Except for telling me to hush, as did everyone else in the reading group. One other thing: She told me to keep my damn hands off her sunburn. Short of a tow truck, nothing would move those people.

"I have a doctorate in physical anthropology with an emphasis on paleopathology, Jerry. That means I do bones and skeletons. Do you know anyone else with my qualifications?" asked Megan, standing up and putting her hands on her hips. I wondered why she had sand on the front of her body. She looked like she had been rolling in a buffalo wallow.

Jerry Carr took a deep breath, then another, looked up at the sky and then at the ground. He was mumbling something, but I couldn't quite catch what he said. I suspect he was counting to fifty since counting to ten doesn't always calm one's temper enough in a discussion with Megan. He turned to the rotund little man whom I assumed was the justice of the peace. "Ed, do I send this skeleton for autopsy?"

Ed the JP scratched his head and looked uncomfortable. "Well, I figure that I can pronounce this here victim dead, being as how he's just skin and bones—heh, heh, heh—but there's no use in sending it to Lubbock for autopsy. There's no meat on them bones, or not too much, just a dried up tendon or two, about enough to connect the thigh bone to the hip bone—heh, heh, heh. If this young lady knows bones, then I reckon we ought to let her look at this poor deceased and see what she finds. She's got a piece of paper that says she's an expert, and we need an expert."

Jerry Carr's face turned red including his ears. "We could ask an anthropologist at the college."

Ryan

Ed the JP straightened his shoulders and stood as tall as he could, which might be two or three inches above Megan's five-two. He should have been a ridiculous figure, but he wasn't. He was imposing; a man in charge—heh, heh, hehs and all. "Lieutenant Carr, I'm the justice of the peace of this precinct, and I have the authority over this crime scene, including the body and any evidence found. Now, since I have this authority I'm going to ask this young lady to examine the victim and ascertain the cause and means of this death."

Jerry Carr, as the cliché goes, was at a loss for words although he was fumbling around for some. He cleared his throat, opened his mouth to speak when the JP held up his hand. "Now, don't argue with me, Lieutenant. I've already made up my mind."

Jerry Carr closed his eyes for a moment, took a deep breath, and nodded.

The JP turned to Megan. "Now, young woman, where do you want these bones taken after you dig them up?"

"To the museum basement, so if I need to consult any books or articles in the course of my examination, I can borrow them from the library or the anthropology department." She turned to Jerry. "Will you call the museum director and ask if I may use a basement workroom with a long table?"

Jerry Carr turned and walked between the members of the reading circle, pulling out a cell phone. I followed him. "Lieutenant, you can't let Megan get involved."

He dialed the museum and spoke a few minutes, then closed his cell phone. "Believe me, Doc, I wish I didn't have to; she's a law-enforcement accident waiting to happen. But you heard the JP. Besides, how can Megan create a problem from what is most probably the skeleton of a missing hiker? Probably had a heart attack or something. The tourists, and even the locals, forget that this canyon gets hot, and you can develop sunstroke before you know it. Or have a heart attack if you're not in too good a shape and think you can hike two or three miles in the heat."

I wondered in the back of my mind why someone would bury an innocent hiker instead of reporting the death, but I was too focused on Megan to worry about it. I shook my head at Jerry Carr's ideas. "No, Lieutenant, Megan is going to create a predicament. It is inevitable. Predicaments and Megan go together like popcorn and movies. I can feel one coming in my bones."

Jerry Carr patted me on the shoulder like I was an old man in need of comfort. "Sit down, Doc, or stand over there with your friends and don't worry about Megan. I can handle the situation."

I swatted his hand away. "If by situation you mean Megan, you haven't handled her the last three times she was involved in a homicide, except for threatening to throw her in jail. And don't call me Doc," I added belatedly.

Agnes took me by the arm, tilted her head back so she could look in my eyes from her height of four feet, ten inches or thereabouts, and drilled me with a laser-guided stare. So far as I know, Agnes never taught school, but she can look at you from those hooded eyes just like a particularly fierce elementary school teacher, the kind who could turn an eight-year-old boy into a mute without saying a word. "Ryan, stand back with me and leave Megan alone. She's been feeling as if life is passing her by, and examining this skeleton will be good for her psyche. She's a brilliant woman who is wasted in Amarillo."

"Wasted? No, she's not!"

She was still looking at me. "Ryan, if she has an opportunity to leave to further her career, you'll let her go, won't you?"

Like the proverbial eight-year-old boy, I was mute. How had Agnes guessed that I felt more for Megan than a man nineteen years older and father of her best friend should? "I think you believe that I have more influence over Megan's decisions than I do. We're just friends."

Agnes hadn't blinked yet. How did she do that? My eyeballs would dry out like raisins and fall out. "And King Henry the Eighth was kind to women."

Feeling unmasked and guilty I stepped back with Agnes to watch Megan do her stuff.

"Has your photographer taken enough pictures for your purposes, Lieutenant?" asked Megan, glancing up at Jerry.

Jerry Carr nodded. "Yeah," he said. He still sounded like he had bitten into a sour lemon. The lieutenant was not a happy camper.

Neither was I.

With a tape measure Megan measured an area four feet square on all four sides of the skeleton, and weighted down crime scene tape with rocks to mark off the boundaries. Then she held her hand out and said, "trowel, please."

Ray Roberts slapped a trowel on Megan's palm as if she was a doctor performing surgery, and in a sense I guess she was. She held her hand out again. "Strainer, please. And Randel, there is a sieve made of screen in a wood frame in the backseat of my pickup. Would you run down and get it for me, please. I'll start with this tea strainer until you get back." Carefully she scooped some of the coarse sand out of the grave and emptied it into the strainer, which she gently shook. A few small objects appeared. All the spectators, including the book club members, leaned as close as we could without actually taking a step. Megan looked up at us and frowned. We straightened up.

Randel jogged up, panting I'm happy to say, and handed Megan the sieve. She dumped the next scoop of dirt into the sieve and shook it. Another few objects appeared. We all leaned forward again. Megan frowned. We straightened up.

She picked up the objects and placed them on a white sheet volunteered by the Special Crimes techs. Then she laid a ruler beside each object and photographed it. The ruler was used so when the pictures were developed, the viewer would know how big each object was. The evidence techs do the same thing when they work a crime scene.

The work progressed slowly. She finally drafted the evidence techs to help, and the police photographer took the pictures. Megan progressed from the trowel to the artists' brushes, and in a couple of instances she used the dental pick. Finally the skeleton was completely uncovered, photographed seven ways to Sunday, and shifted onto the white sheet where its portrait was taken again. The skeleton was pretty much complete except for a few finger bones. The rib cage and arm bones were jumbled from Rembrandt's and Horatio's tug of war with the shirt, but Megan found all of them. She didn't find all the finger bones. Animals carried them off was her guess. It helped that our skinny friend was wearing Levis which helped keep together the bones below the waist. The skeleton wore no shoes, but Megan found all the tiny bones of the foot except two distal phalanges (toe bones) of the right foot. In plain English, the end bone of the big toe, and the end bone of the third toe. That's what distal means, the end bone of the toes where the toenail is.

After sunset Special Crimes set up battery-operated portable lights so the work could continue. The reading club members stayed, although most of us were sitting now instead of standing. The search was nearly done. Megan told me later that when excavating a skeleton, one always dug for a certain distance away on all sides of the bones, in this case, four feet. I was tired; I think all of us were tired except Megan and Special Crimes. They were used to working long hours collecting evidence, measuring, and photographing.

Falángees

The last scoop of dirt, which was taken from the outer edge of the dig area, at a depth of approximately three feet yielded several small bones. Megan placed them on the white sheet and the photographer did his thing with camera and ruler. I thought we, or Megan rather, were done, until she looked up at Jerry Carr. "I want a flashlight, Jerry, a really bright one."

"Why do you need a flashlight? You've got four really bright portable lights."

Megan snapped her fingers and held out her hand, while looking closely at the most recent bones found. "Light, please, Jerry."

Jerry sighed in exasperation but handed her a large flashlight. "Lieutenant Roberts," she said to the retired police officer. "Hand me that magnifying glass, please."

Megan's voice vibrated just slightly as it was in the soprano range instead of its usual alto. Although there was little or no expression on her face, Megan's voice gave away her excitement. She examined the four tiny objects she found with the magnifying glass while Lieutenant Roberts held the flashlight, directing its beam directly on the objects. The rest of us were holding our breath.

Megan moved to the skeleton and placed the two missing distals on the end of the big toe and the third toe of the right foot. She stood up and stretched, holding the other two objects in her hand. "Jerry, you can wrap the skeleton in the sheet and put it in the body bag. Then I'll want another white sheet and more crime scene tape. And, Lieutenant Roberts, be ready with my tape measure, please."

"Are you going dig farther out from the grave?" asked Jerry Carr, running his hands through his hair. I had seen him do that before when trying to deal with Megan during a homicide investigation. He was usually trying to persuade her to keep her nose out of his business. This time she was involved up to her eyeballs, and I wasn't sure Jerry Carr was going to survive with any of his hair left.

She walked the few feet to Jerry Carr and shone the flashlight on the two objects in her hand. "I said I was missing two distal phalanges. I found them as you can see from the skeleton."

falanges

Jerry looked at our skinny—and mostly skinless—friend on the white sheet. "Okay, I see them. So what do you want to show me?"

Megan looked up at him. "These are two distal phalanges from a left foot."

Jerry peered at the skeleton for a moment. "But the skeleton has the same bones on its left foot as it has on its right foot."

"That's right."

"You telling me that one of Mr. Bony's feet is deformed and has extra toes? That would really make it easier to identify him. Not many people have two extra toe nails."

Megan shook her head. "These two bones don't belong to that skeleton."

Jerry Carr blinked a few times, a confused expression on his face before he shook his head in denial. "Oh, no, my God, no, Megan. You're not saying what I think you're saying. Are you?"

"I'm saying there is another skeleton—right there!" she exclaimed, pointing to a spot just on the other side of the crime scene tape, about four feet to the right of the first skeleton's grave.

"My God!" said Randel. "It's a dump site! It must be a serial killer. I'll bet there are bodies buried all around here." I noticed that Randel had lost his phony English accent.

damn

"I feel just like I'm in one of those crime-scene-investigation TV programs," said Rosemary Pittman with a shiver of excitement.

"Just a minute!" yelled Jerry Carr, but it was too late. One of the Special Crimes techs had laid down another white sheet, while the rest of the techs and Megan were already scooping the gritty sand into the sieve which Lieutenant Roberts was shaking.

"Damn it, I said just a minute! Megan is jumping to conclusions!" yelled Jerry Carr.

Everybody ignored him and kept digging. Even the book club members were digging using their hands. Even I was digging. You could feel the tension humming in the air like an electrical high wire.

Megan suddenly stopped in the middle of scooping up some sand. "Lieutenant Roberts, please hand me those brushes, please."

Everyone else stopped, too. We sat back on our heels and watched and waited while Megan brushed away sand with a three-inch paintbrush. Gradually, a round object appeared. It was covered with the remains of a trade blanket, the kind that Amerindians traded for during the nineteenth century, or were given to the Indians by the government. The blanket was hardly more than scraps of wool yarn, so Megan brushed them aside using a small, soft artists' brush. A skull appeared. Let me rephrase that. It was a skull covered with mummified skin. Stubby eyelashes remained, but the hair was only patchy black wisps. Megan lifted away the rest of the blanket, and scraped away sand from its torso to gradually reveal a body in a dried white buckskin dress with fringe on the sleeves and decorated with red beads. The white hide moccasin had fallen off its left foot to reveal two missing distal phalanges. Its mummified arms were folded over its chest, and something black was laced between the fingers which were held together with dried tendons. There was no sound at all except a soft breeze blowing through the wild plum trees. The leaves barely rustled. There

falánges

was a hush, a sense of suspended movement, as if the canyon itself watched Megan gently, reverently stroke the mummy's cheek. I heard what I thought was a sob behind me. I turned to offer my handkerchief to whoever was so softhearted as to cry over a mummy, but I saw no one crying.

Megan twisted on her knees to face me. All the excitement missing from her face before was there now. "Isn't it wonderful, Ryan? Not only do I have bones, I also have a mummy!"

Native

6

You don't have much hope of getting the truth, if you
think you know in advance what the truth ought to be.

—Spenser in Robert B. Parker's
Pale Kings and Princes, 1987

PALO DURO CANYON, 1868

Fat Belly stood at the canyon's mouth just as Spotted
Tongue had asked which didn't surprise him. Fat Belly
might be a clown sometimes, but he was a warrior, too, and
wouldn't break his word.

"Fat Belly, my friend, I thank you," said Spotted Tongue,
leading his pony. Not to ride was another sacrifice for Little
Flower. A member of the People practically lived on horse-
back. To voluntarily walk when one could ride was a sign
of mourning nearly as powerful as cutting off his braids.
He tried to smile at Fat Belly, but grimaced instead. He had
no humor, no reassurance in him. "Let's go back to our
camp so you can sleep."

Staring at Spotted Tongue's lack of braids Fat Belly
gasped with horror. "You've cut off your braids! Had Little
Flower so stolen your wits that you would mutilate yourself
like that?"

Spotted Tongue frowned at Fat Belly's assumption that
he was so weak that a woman could lead him around like

he led his ponies. He was angry that his friend saw cutting off his braids as a mutilation. Did no one understand his deep sorrow? Was he the only warrior to hold a woman close to his heart and feel his spirit cast down when she was gone? "I must show her spirit how much sorrow I felt, for I loved her more than life. Did you ever love a woman like that, Fat Belly?"

Fat Belly looked at him strangely. "You loved a woman more than your ponies?"

Spotted Tongue knew at one time he would have felt the same. He knew better now. "Ponies and women aren't the same. I would never cut off my braids if my favorite pony died. I'd feel sad, then go steal another horse."

Fat Belly shook his head, a pitying expression on his face. "Things are not right with your wits, Spotted Tongue. You need to make strong medicine again because the medicine you have now has failed you."

Spotted Tongue nodded but forced his words back into throat. He couldn't tell Fat Belly that his medicine failed him long ago and visions had deserted him. His people might think he had broken many taboos and exile him before he brought evil. "I'll think on your words, Fat Belly. Now go sleep in your arbor while it's still cool."

Fat Belly yawned and rubbed his stomach, Spotted Tongue's strange behavior dismissed from his mind. "Not until I eat. I'll starve when food is scarce so the children can eat, but there isn't need now. There's plenty of buffalo left from the last hunt. The women should have the fires built so our wives can roast us a piece, a big piece. I could eat a whole buffalo by myself. I have to feed myself to keep this strong, handsome body." He laughed at himself as he lifted his belly off his breechclout. "This is where I carry my strength." He threw his arm over Spotted Tongue's shoulder. "So, my friend, let's feast and sleep."

Spotted Tongue swallowed the bile that rose in his throat at the thought of food. "I'll not sleep today. Until I punish Little Flower's murderer, I will find no rest."

"You think you know who it is?" asked Fat Belly, his face expressionless.

Spotted Tongue clasped his friend's arm to stop him. "Who hated her most in camp, Fat Belly? Who beat her when I was gone hunting or tending to my ponies?"

Fat Belly searched Spotted Tongue's face, then sighed. "You think that Green Willow killed her?"

Spotted Tongue nodded. "I fear so, for who else would it be? She and Little Flower went together to pick the wild plums. Green Willow returned alone."

Fat Belly squeezed his friend's shoulder. "Surely you'll not kill Green Willow over a slave. I liked her, and her beauty would blind a man or make him foolish, but to kill Green Willow . . . I don't know that you ought to do that, Spotted Tongue."

Spotted Tongue felt his heart pound with frustration. Would he always hear that Little Flower was a slave? "She was my second wife! That means she was a Nerm by adoption and not a slave. Spilling the blood of a Nerm is against the ways of the Nermernuh, but when murder happens, as it did to Little Flower, I'm allowed by custom to hunt down the murderer and kill her without interference and without her family swearing revenge. And I will have retribution!" He pounded his right fist against his opposing palm.

Fat Belly grabbed his hands. "Calm yourself, my friend. Next you'll be cutting off the ends of your fingers as women do when they mourn. I've never seen such great sorrow, Spotted Tongue, as you suffer. I've never seen a warrior cut off his braids over the death of anyone, but especially not a woman. The most a man sacrifices is a patch of hair, but to sacrifice your braids, I've not even heard of such a thing.

Little Flower's spirit knows how deeply you mourn her. Is it necessary to kill Green Willow? Could you not beat her instead? And are you sure that Green Willow is guilty? Sometimes we think we know something, but our minds are clouded and we're wrong. Don't accuse Green Willow yet, not until you make medicine and ask advice of your animal spirit. Come with me instead. I'll tell my wife to cook us both some buffalo and we'll have some of the plums she picked. You eat until your belly is as big and strong as mine. Then you sleep, my friend, sleep away the clouds in your mind, so you might see clearly."

Spotted Tongue closed his eyes to shut out the sight of his friend's worried face. He wanted to laugh bitterly at the warrior's advice. He could make no medicine nor could he call on his animal spirit. The spirit of the wolf no longer answered his prayers. He opened his eyes. "No, Fat Belly. I must confront Green Willow before I can eat or sleep. Otherwise, the food would sour my stomach, and sleep would bring nightmares, not rest. You go ahead and tell your wife to feed you well. I'll follow after I ask a blessing."

Fat Belly switched his lance to his other hand. As all lances that warriors of the Nermernuh carried, Fat Belly's was fourteen feet long and felt awkward and heavy after a time. "You remember what I said, Spotted Tongue. Think on what you do. Green Willow is the only woman you gave a pony herd for, and a big herd at that. Everyone thought bad medicine had destroyed your wits to give so many ponies for a woman when there were many other good and beautiful women you could have had for fewer ponies. Will you kill her now when you know she is such a hard worker? She can take down a tipi faster than any woman. She can put one up faster, too. She can cut up a buffalo into pieces for cooking faster than the other women. And she can soften buckskin and make you moccasins and shirts to wear when

*the snows come. You're the only man in the band who has
two extra shirts and two extra pairs of moccasins besides
what you wear, and she managed all that before you captured Little Flower to help her. Would you kill a good
woman like her when you didn't see her murder Little
Flower, and you don't know if anyone else saw her, either?
You're like a man who hears a sound in the dark and thinks
an enemy is trying to get into his tipi, so he stabs him. But
it's not an enemy at all, it's his wife who went outside to
make water." Fat Belly clapped him on his shoulder. "Think
on what I said, Spotted Tongue."*

Spotted Tongue watched Fat Belly cross the stream, pick
up one of the children playing at being a warrior, and swing
him around and around, laughing all the while. Why
couldn't life be so good for him as it was for Fat Belly? Why
couldn't he make medicine anymore? Had the spirits cursed
him by taking away his belief? If Fat Belly learned of it,
would he still be a friend, or would he be afraid instead.

Pushing his thoughts away to worry about later, Spotted
Tongue wrapped his pony's reins around his wrist, lifted
his arms, and tilted his head to the eastern sky where the
sun rose over the canyon wall in a burst of yellow and red
and orange. He repeated his actions, facing the other three
directions. He felt no blessing, no comfort. He fell to his
knees, bowed his head, and pulled at his hair. He was alone
among the Nermernuh, as far away from being a Nerm as if
his existence were no more than a reflection in clear water.

He rose from the ground and led his pony across the
stream. He removed the reins and whispered, "run, boy,
back to your friends." He stepped away and watched the
pony lope away toward the southern end of the canyon.
There wasn't need to slap the pony or to scream at it. The
ponies of the Nermernuh were raised and trained by love.
They obeyed because they loved the men who rode them.

He turned toward the camp and saw Green Willow roasting buffalo meat in front of his brush arbor. She cooked a large piece of buffalo meat pierced by a sharp stick. The stick rested on a spit built of two forked sticks pushed into the ground on either side of the fire. Green Willow turned the meat to cook each side. Spotted Tongue smelled the juices dripping on the fire and felt nauseated.

Green Willow looked up at him when he stopped by her. "Will you have meat, Spotted Tongue?"

Spotted Tongue studied her face but couldn't detect any fear. Only her eyes darted this way and that to avoid looking at him. "I'm not hungry."

Green Willow turned the meat again. "I have plums that I picked. Would you like some? They're very sweet this year."

"I want no plums."

She sat back on her heels and finally looked into his eyes. She licked her lips and rested her hands on her thighs. There was a nervous quiver in her voice when she spoke. "Did you find her?"

"Yes, I found her."

"She didn't come back with you?"

"No, nor will she ever."

She looked confused. "Why? Did you let her go free? Is she staying up in the canyon until you return? That's where you were last night? With her? I saw you riding that way with a blanket, and a good thing, too. She doesn't like dirt and is always washing her hands and face. She would even take off her clothes and wash herself all over whenever we camped by water. I told her that she couldn't wash all over when the snows blew or she would get the disease that steals your breath."

"I didn't let her go, but I did stay with her last night. And I know she doesn't like to be dirty."

"If you're not staying up there with her again tonight,

then I want her here. She can help me cut the rest of the buffalo into thin strips and mash them together with the plums and mustang grapes. And she can break the shells of the pecans and walnuts we picked before we came to the canyon. With two people the work can go much faster. And I'll try to teach her our tongue again, but Spotted Tongue, I thinks she lacks the wits to learn."

"Exactly where did you leave Little Flower?"

She answered the question with a question. "Why do you need to know? Spotted Tongue, what is the matter? Have your wits fled? Or you just don't want to talk?"

He put his hands under her arms and lifted her to her feet. "Stand up! Now answer my question. Where exactly did you leave Little Flower?"

She put her hands on his chest to push him away, but she might as well have pushed a big tree. "I left her by that large rock."

Spotted Tongue released her and stepped back. "Who was with her?"

"Spotted Tongue, what is this all about? What has Little Flower done that makes you act like—well, like Coyote Dung? He jerks his wife around like she was a captive slave instead of a Nerm."

He raised his hand, and she flinched. "Answer my question!" he shouted.

Tears glistened in her eyes. "Coyote Dung hits his wife, too."

Spotted Tongue felt guilty; worse than that, he felt touched by evil. He rubbed his hand over his face like he could wipe away that temptation to do evil. He felt compelled to apologize to Green Willow and finally found the words. "I'm sorry, Green Willow. I won't hit you, but I want you to answer my question."

"There were several women, including Buffalo Woman and Fat Belly's woman, Slow Like a Turtle. I can't remember who else."

"Who among those women was still there when you left?"

"The ones I named!"

"Why would they hurt Little Flower?" asked Spotted Tongue, his suspicion growing again. *"I know that almost every slave is abused by other women, but abuse is one thing, and murder is another."*

Green Willow flinched away, a hand on either cheek and a look of horror in her eyes. *"By the spirit of the Cannibal Owl. None of the Nermernuh would commit murder, Spotted Tongue. Little Flower was your property—and your wife. They would know they would have to pay you if they murdered her."*

"So none of those women would murder Little Flower?"

"No, Spotted Tongue, they would have no reason to murder her. What harm could she do to them?"

Spotted Tongue stepped closer to her, a feeling of dread in his chest. *"Who among the women in our band would have a reason to murder her, Green Willow?"*

At first she looked thoughtful, then a look of fear gradually appeared on her face as she saw the suspicion in his eyes. *"No, Spotted Tongue!"* she cried, cringing away. *"I didn't kill her! Hold a burning stick to my body if you think I'm lying. I'll still say no."*

"But you admit that you're the only woman with reason to kill her?"

"No! Oh, I admit I got so angry with her because she refused to understand. And sometimes she would look at me as if she was a Nerm and I was the dirt she walked upon. Sometimes I was so jealous, Spotted Tongue. You were her

captive instead of the other way around. She would look into your eyes and draw your spirit out. You couldn't be near without touching her, and you didn't seem to care that she tried to pull away from you."

Grief twisted Spotted Tongue's heart. That he could never again touch Little Flower was almost more than he could bear. "She only pulled away when you were near, Green Willow. Did it ever occur to you that Little Flower knew you were jealous and didn't want to hurt you? If she acted as if my touch was like poison to her, you wouldn't feel so jealous. She might refuse to speak our tongue or to understand us, but she knew you were first wife and had first claim. She wasn't witless. She learned our customs and knew that my attentions to her made you feel threatened. And she shared my tipi from the moment I brought her back to camp, but that was my choice. I don't know that she looked at you like you were dirt. She was a proud woman, and not bowing her head was one way to save her pride." He didn't tell her that there were times, when Little Flower was very sad, or she was ill, that she didn't avoid his touch. There were times he brought her much pleasure. He didn't know why she cried afterwards.

Green Willow covered her face with her hands and rocked back and forth. She began the keening sound of grief. She took away her hands and looked at him. "I hated her sometimes and I was jealous, but other times we would sit in the sun and sew and there would be peace between us. And once—once she smiled at me. We were near the salt fork of the Red River. The grass and trees were greening and the early flowers were blooming. We came to a bend in the river and the flowers spread out like many giant beads spilled on the ground. She laughed and picked a flower. She smelled it, but those flowers sometimes don't smell sweet. She wrinkled her nose and looked over at me and smiled."

Green Willow swallowed and wiped her hands on her skirt. Tears were making tracks down her cheeks. "I never thought she might be acting like she hated for you to touch her so I wouldn't feel unhappy. I'm sorry I hated her and I'm sorry I hit her so much. She was your second wife and I should have honored you by welcoming her. But she was so different from us!"

She pulled the knife she carried and slashed her arms while screaming her grief.

Spotted Tongue grabbed her wrist and twisted it until she dropped the knife. "You will not cut yourself. I forbid it! I know it's the custom for women of the Nermernuh to mutilate themselves to show their grief, but I've seen poison get into their bodies through the cuts on their arms and legs and breasts. The wounds would swell and began to rot and the women would die. Sometimes the wounds would fill with worms and the women would also die. I will not risk your dying such a death. Pack your wounds with grass and bind them."

The other members of the band ran toward Spotted Tongue's brush arbor, curious as to the cause of the screaming. Spotted Tongue heard the murmurs behind them, and led Green Willow into his arbor where politeness dictated that they be left alone. They waited until everyone returned to their own arbors.

"Did you murder Little Flower?"

Green Willow, face streaked with tears and with blood running down her arms, looked at him. "I did not, Spotted Tongue."

He studied her eyes looking for truth. He saw fear beginning to grow instead. He had noticed since he lost his medicine that women and warriors alike couldn't meet his eyes for long without fearing him. He didn't know what they saw except that he was a stranger in their midst. He *didn't know of a single person who could lie to him now.*

Green Willow began to cry. "I didn't murder Little Flower. I swear it."

Spotted Tongue believed her.

NotRyan

7

*The world winked at secret vices as long as there was
an attempt at concealment, though it was cruelly severe on those which were brought to light.*

—Felix Rolleston in Fergus Hume's
The Mystery of a Hansom Cab, 1886

AMARILLO, TEXAS, PRESENT DAY

newslike

BURIAL SITES FOUND
IN PALO DURO CANYON
by James Timmons

AMARILLO, TEXAS—A picnic lunch ended
on a note of horror yesterday for a local mystery readers' club. According to a source in the
Randall County Sheriff's Office, Dr. Megan
Clark was walking her two dogs in Little Sunday Canyon after sharing a picnic lunch with
the other members of the Murder by the Yard
Reading Circle, when her two beagles slipped
their leashes. The two animals began fighting
over a scrap of cloth at the base of Indian
Rock. When Dr. Clark caught up with her two
dogs she discovered that the scrap was part of
a shirt worn by a skeleton.

Dr. Clark, who claims to be a physical anthropologist, was appointed by Justice of the Peace Ed Hagan to excavate and examine the skeleton. Before one could say the thigh bone is connected to the hip bone, Dr. Clark discovered extra toe bones, which she believed belonged to another skeleton. Dr. Clark was right and she was wrong. There were remains buried next to the first grave, but it was not a skeleton. Instead, Dr. Clark excavated a female mummy dressed in a well-preserved buckskin dress and moccasins.

According to Dr. Norman Ryland, a curator at the Panhandle-Plains Museum in Canyon, Texas, Palo Duro Canyon was the winter campground of the Quahadi Comanches. "Although remains have been discovered in Palo Duro Canyon before, we have never found a Comanche mummy. We have much to learn from this mummy, and as a curator with a special interest in Native Americans I will require access to the remains, so that an accurate assessment may be made of its historical significance. We at the museum appreciate Dr. Clark's efforts to determine the age of the mummy, but the significance of any possible artifacts found in the grave needs, of course, examination by experts."

Phone calls made to Dr. Clark's home went unanswered. The director of the Amarillo Public Library where Dr. Clark is an assistant librarian refused to comment on the whereabouts of the self-proclaimed anthropologist. Jerry Carr of Special Crimes stated that information about the skeleton and the Comanche mummy will be released as soon as Dr. Clark completes her examination. He refused to answer questions about Dr. Clark's inclusion in a police press conference."

not Ryan

Megan, dressed in sterile surgical scrubs, paper booties, paper hair covering, and a mask, stood in the middle of Potter County's brand-new, fully equipped morgue, tearing the morning *Amarillo Globe-News* into tiny pieces, dropping them on the floor, and stomping on them in time with a single word chanted to a tune of her own: "Damn, damn, damn, damndamndamn, damn, damn, damn. . . ."

Ryan The door opened and Ryan walked in, stopped, and watched Megan's dance. "You know, the Comanches before their culture was cross-pollinated by the culture of damn near every other tribe on the High Plains, and even some of the southwestern pueblo myths, had only one socializing ritual: the war dance. Each warrior made up his own steps, much as you are doing. They stomped, leaped, chanted, jumped, wiggled, swayed, and shouted in time to the music of a hide drum, while the women stood outside the circle and cheered their men on. Since I don't happen to have a hide drum on me, your repetition of the word 'damn' chanted to that catchy little tune ought to do. Watching you I can imagine you in buckskin and moccasins. . . ."

ah Megan whirled around and frowned at him, and his voice trailed away. She hated it when Ryan slipped into his professorial guise. Not that his lectures weren't interesting, but he always chose to deliver them when she had something else on her mind. Sometimes she believed he knew when she was worried or angry, and lectured to take her mind off whatever was bothering her.

It always irritated the devil out of her.

Ryan cleared his throat and changed the subject. "I've been driving all over two counties trying to find you. I first went to the museum, but Dr. Ryland said you had changed your mind about working in the basement. Then I called Jerry Carr and he told me where you were. Reluctantly, but he did tell me."

"Ryan . . ."

"I see you read the paper this morning."

"Are you trying to be funny?"

"Not when you're frowning like that. Remember your mother always says that you'll have wrinkles at an early age if you don't stop frowning."

"I have to listen to my mother when she tells me that. I don't have to listen to you." She drew a deep breath and pointed to the floor. "Did you read that article about the remains?"

"Yes, I did, and I called the paper to complain about the few errors I found. The columnist ought to check his sources more carefully," said Ryan as rapidly as he could to distract Megan from the subject of her tirade.

"A few errors! Did you say a few errors? Did you see where he said I claimed to be an anthropologist? *Claimed!* Like I was a liar! And stating that the mummy is a Comanche! I haven't verified the mummy's race, but I have a pretty good idea what it is just by checking out the features. But I haven't made a final decision, so where does that pompous ass get off announcing race without asking me?"

Megan kicked at the pieces of paper and paced the perimeter of the morgue, swinging her arms and chanting again. "Damn, damn, damn, and double damn."

She could sense Ryan's debating whether to say anything in Dr. Ryland's defense and deciding against it by the expression on his face. Ryan was very perceptive. Ryland was an ass.

Megan stopped in front of Ryan. "And did you see where he demanded *access* to the mummy because poor little me with my Ph.D. in physical anthropology is too dumb to make a decision about any burial goods in the grave. And by the way, when did he become the expert on the Amerindians? You're the curator of history with a Ph.D. and wrote a brilliant dissertation on the origin and dispersal of the Amerindians prior to the arrival of the Spanish. And you did postgraduate work on the confrontation between the horse Indians and the white man, with the Comanche as the prototype of the horse Indian."

She made another circuit of the room and stopped in front of Ryan again. "And while I'm dissecting Dr. Ryland, there is something else that irks me. Calling Amerindians Native Americans! That is a label thought up by some bureaucrat at the Census department or office or bureau or however it's listed on the federal government's organizational chart. A Native American is anyone born in America. I hate it when a bureaucrat assigns an inaccurate meaning to a perfectly understood term. Amerindian specifically means an ethnic Indian indigenous to the United States and Canada, except for the Aleuts and Inuits. It is a more specific term than Native Americans in my opinion, which is worth at least as much as a Washington bureaucrat's. Either term lumps all the tribes together like they are identical peas in a pod. They aren't! Each tribe has major or minor differences. There are numerous language groups and dialects. A Comanche has a vastly different culture than a Zuni or a Sioux. Or the Comanche used to have a vastly different culture before they were moved onto the reservation to be mixed and matched with the cultures of other Plains tribes. A great many changes came about thanks to Easterners with a preconceived notion of what a Plains Indian was supposed to look like. And I know that because I'm an anthropologist and am required to have at least a small working knowledge of the major ethnic groups. And I reread all my anthropology textbooks last night, as well as two general, but thorough, books my mother had on the Comanche."

Megan stopped, drew a breath, took a drink from her bottled water, and continued. "So why does that arrogant, pompous, ill-informed ignoramus insinuate that I barely know enough to put on my clothes in the morning and speak in complete sentences? And why is he trying to pre-empt your field of expertise?"

Ryan cleared his throat. "Because he is an arrogant, pompous, ill-informed ignoramus who can't imagine that a twenty-six-year-old woman knows more than he does. Forget him, Megan. And forget the article. You have too much important work to do examining your finds to allow someone like Dr. Ryland to upset you."

Megan sniffed and hoped she didn't start crying again out of sheer frustration and fury. "But everyone in town will think that I'm a liar and a doofus."

Ryan leaned against a cabinet and grinned at her. "Since when do you care what the neighbors think?"

She grinned back and plucked two surgical gloves from a box. "Never. Now put that lab coat on and grab one of those masks out of the third drawer on your left. Oh, and put on one of those caps like mine. And surgical gloves. I want you to wear surgical gloves. The mummy might contain microorganisms of some kind that it's probably best not to inhale or get on your hands."

She pulled on her gloves, wiggled her fingers at him, and walked to the first gurney. "Come on, Professor. Let's get started. We'll do the skeleton first. I can't imagine that I'll have any questions about it that you can answer. But the mummy! I'm sure you'll have some valuable observations on her clothes, etc., that you can share with me."

Megan cut off the skeleton's Levis and what the dogs had left of its shirt. She examined the remaining buttons on the shirt and started humming. She emptied the pockets in both articles of clothes. The shirt pocket was empty, but the Levis revealed gold. She held up some coins. "Look what I found, Ryan! Now we can get some idea of how old this skeleton is."

"How will coins help us?"

Megan looked up from studying the coins. "Dates, Ryan, dates. The most recent date on any of these coins is five years ago. It's hard to say exactly how old bones are with any exactness unless you can date artifacts found with the remains. Coins will give the oldest possible date of the remains, so we know our skeleton was still a living, breathing human being five years ago. When I examine the bones I might be able to narrow that time period a bit."

She tucked the two items of clothes into a paper bag and dated it and initialed it. The evidence tech would examine the clothes for any foreign hair or fiber or blood, but she had nothing else to do with the clothes. Then she measured the long bones in the leg and arm, reading numbers into the microphone, then entering them into a calculator and performing several functions. She whistled as she worked like one of Snow White's dwarfs. She tried to remember when she had last whistled and couldn't.

Megan smiled at Ryan. "Our lady was thirty-five to thirty-nine-years-old when she died, according to my examination of the degree of bone growth. In other words, all the bones that should have fused together, have done so. I also examined the extent of arthritis in the joints of the knee, hip, shoulder, and elbow. Our lady showed the beginning of arthritis in those joints, but not to a great degree, so I judged her to be middle to late thirties. Oh, and she stood five foot six to five foot eight but had small bones for her size. As you might guess I've already done an extensive examination, but I'll show you how I came to my various conclusions."

"She?" asked Ryan. "You already know she was female?"

"All right, Dr. Pompous Ass. Of course, I already know it's female and it is most likely an American female, and I've had a lot of experience determining gender in an American population. Feel the upper margin of the orbit—the hole where the eye goes, Ryan. Feel how sharp it is? Most females have this sharp edge as opposed to males who have a relatively blunt edge. The skull is relatively smooth as opposed to rugged or coarse in males. The skull of the female is smaller than that of a male and generally has a small, pointed rather than square chin. The female has a rounded and full forehead, a small palate generally shaped like a parabola, and lighter, more curved cheek bones as opposed to heavier with a more lateral arch in males. The brow ridges are not terribly prominent in a female, as these aren't. Some males have brow ridges that resemble those of a Neanderthal. You could practically set a coffee cup on their brow ridges.

"The last, and to my mind the most, defining characteristic is the pelvis. The superior aperture is larger and more rounded. The superior aperture in a male is smaller and heart-shaped. In other words, if you find the pelvis to have female characteristics, and the characteristics found in the face—chin, forehead, brow ridges, pointed chin, etc.—also indicate a female, then you have a female, period."

Megan pointed out each location of each characteristic on the skull as she described it. "There are other indicators, but I'm going to skip pointing those out to you. I have checked them and have judged that each indicates a female. Now, let's go on to race. Our lady has a Caucasoid skull which means she is white. Her cheekbones do not extend forward; the nasal aperture is narrow and has a dam or nasal sill; and she has a flat face in the dental area along the midline of the face. Also, she has a long, narrow face and a narrow, high-bridged nose. A Mongoloid skull which includes Amerindians, has a flat, round face with the cheekbones protruding forward and dipping below the lower edges of the upper jaw. That's why, if you look at nineteenth-century photographs of Amerindians, the cheekbones are the most prominent feature. However, there has been so much intermarriage between whites and Amerindians that it is becoming difficult sometimes to assign race, so you might have a mixed blood with Caucasoid cheekbones."

"The defining characteristics of an Amerindian face in my opinion is the edge-to-edge bite. That means when you hold the jaws closed the teeth meet instead of exhibiting an overbite which is usually found in Caucasoids or Negroids."

Ryan looked solemn. "Agnes was right. You are wasted in Amarillo."

Megan blinked in surprise. She didn't realize that her friends picked up on her feelings that life and career opportunities were passing her by. "I would leave if I could find work in my field. If I move and end up gluing together broken pottery in a museum basement somewhere, I might as well stay here. At least I don't have to pay rent." She smiled at Ryan and pulled on a new pair of surgical gloves. "Shall we move on to the mummy?"

"Wait a minute! You didn't tell me how our Miss Bony died," said Ryan, not moving away from the gurney.

Megan shrugged her shoulders. "Oh, she was murdered. I found the knife marks on her rib cage, her breastbone, and one on a vertebra. Someone wanted to make very sure she was dead."

Megan moved over to another table and removed the sheet that covered the mummy. "Here she is! Miss

Comanche. Who do you suppose she was, Ryan? Whoever killed her was a coward because she was killed by blunt-force trauma to the back of the skull. In other words, someone sneaked up on her." She gently patted the mummy's clasped hands as if reassuring her of something. "I stopped at the library this morning and checked out several books, including T. R. Fehrenbach's work on the Comanches and *Indian Depredations in Texas* by J.W. Wilbarger. It was first published in 1889 and Miss Comanche was a captive before 1875 when the last band of Comanches surrendered."

"Why go to all that effort, Megan? You'll never know who she is."

Megan looked. "I have to try, Ryan. A Comanche warrior loved her very much because he cut off his braids as a sign of mourning and buried her with them clasped in her hands. According to Fehrenbach, Comanche warriors were very vain about their braids and spent a lot of time braiding their hair, adding feathers and shells and whatever beautiful objects they had. For a warrior to cut off his braids to mourn a woman represents such a gesture of love that I can't even describe it."

She touched the mummy's skull. "Yet someone hated her enough to murder her. Such love and such hate, Ryan. Between the two extremes there is a story, and I want to know as much of that story as possible."

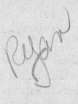

8

Murders are about love . . . If you were a cynic you might even say they are the purest expression of it. Love—for a man or a woman, for money, revenge, religion, or even love of one's self. One way or another, all murders are crimes of passion.

—Detective-Inspector Ben Jurnet
in S.T. Haymon's *Stately Homicide,* 1984

AMARILLO, TEXAS, PRESENT DAY

I followed Megan to the Special Crimes offices, so she could give her report to Jerry Carr. Ordinarily I ride with Megan or she rides with me, but since we had driven out to the morgue separately, I missed the nervous stomach that usually accompanies riding with her. Not that I'm going to miss a burning stomach entirely. Just as I predicted, Megan has precipitated a predicament that will necessitate my replenishing my supply of antacid. As usual, she plans on lending a hand in investigating the murder of our Miss Bony, and as usual, she told me about it. But I don't even get a decent role in one of her predicaments. The Dr. Watson I play isn't the Dr. Watson who is a dignified partner to the principal sleuth. No, I always play the role of sidekick, the comic relief. No wonder I'm afraid to hint to Megan that my feelings have changed from platonic love to a deeper, more mature, romantic love that has raised my water bill significantly due to the number of cold showers I average every day. Who wants to date the comic relief?

I picked up my argument where I left off when we rode together in the elevator to Jerry Carr's office. "Megan, you're an anthropologist slash paleopathologist. You're not a detective with Special Crimes. You've had three close calls in a row playing amateur sleuth, and three's a charm. You're not a cat, you don't have nine lives. The fourth time you stick your nose into one of Jerry Carr's murder investigations, you're going to get it chopped off."

The elevator opened onto a featureless hall and we turned and walked down another long hall to a reception area where a secretary sat behind a large desk. We had been reluctant guests of Special Crimes so many times that I even knew the names of the secretary's children. I sat down to watch the fish in the enormous aquarium and let Megan talk to the secretary. I had made friends with one of the fish by the time Megan had talked her way into an immediate appointment with the lieutenant. Watching fish is a restful way to pass the time and let your stomach settle.

Jerry Carr's office is small, maybe eight by eight or ten by ten, in which is stuffed a desk, a tall legal-sized filing cabinet, Jerry's chair, and a chair for guests. The guest chair was occupied which was all right with me. Those cheap, formed plastic, government-issued chairs always leave my buttocks numb. I'd rather hold up the wall.

Jerry's visitor rose and held out his hand. "You must be the Dr. Clark I read about in the paper this morning. I'm glad I have an opportunity to speak with you before I arrange to take custody of the Comanche mummy under the Native American Grave Protection and Repatriation Act. I find it necessary to explain to the archaeologists and anthropologists who feel their museums or their universities should keep Native American remains for scientific study, that they wouldn't want their ancestors' bodies dug up and put on display anymore than Native Americans do."

Megan stood there looking at him as if she would like to put him on display in a glass case. "Who are you?"

"This is Gray Wolf Murphy, a Comanche shaman who is conducting rituals for those Comanches in Oklahoma who invite him," said the lieutenant in a monotone.

I couldn't stand it. I had to ask. "What kind of ritual, Mr. Murphy?" I asked in a voice I hoped expressed doubt. He looked startled that I asked such a question. I guess he wasn't used to explaining to a skeptic.

"We will have a sun dance, and of course I will use my medicine to bless the homes of the participants."

"I believe that the Comanches adopted the sun dance from the Kiowa after 1780. It didn't originate with the Comanches," I said. "And the Comanches never mutilated themselves by being raised off the ground by means of rawhide thongs tied to wooden skewers thrust through the skin and muscles of their backs or chests, the *okipa*. Although sometimes the Comanche warrior would outline a war scar with tatoos, he would never deliberately mutilate himself. Unsightly scars or mutilations were the result of accident or war. The Comanche warrior was a vain individual. And the Comanche didn't take the sun dance very seriously anyway. They had very few rituals and the only one that was important to them was the war dance performed before leaving for a raid. It was a warrior culture. Every ritual, every event paled in comparison to war.

Gray Wolf Murphy's very white skin turned pink. "Who are you?"

"Dr. Ryan Stevens, curator of history at the Panhandle-Plains Museum."

"I seem to be surrounded by scholars. We can never have

enough knowledge." Evidently thinking that he had his fill of conversation with me, he turned to Megan. "I have already spoken to one of your local funeral directors, and he has agreed to accompany me to wherever the mummy is for the purpose of placing the remains in a casket for transfer to Oklahoma after I've made medicine and called upon the spirit of the buffalo to cleanse and to bless our Comanche ancestor. I'm sure my tribal council will agree with me that burial next to Chief Quanah Parker and his family would be appropriate."

Megan stepped away from the wall. I had been watching her cheeks darken from light pink to red. I don't know what the color red signifies in the rest of the world, or even the rest of the country, but when Megan's cheeks turn red, it means stop *now*. It means that a kevlar flak jacket and helmet is recommended.

"Mr. Murphy, you are making an assumption based on false information. I didn't say that the mummy is Comanche or even an Amerindian. It is not. She was white, she was pregnant, she was a captive, and she was murdered by blunt force trauma." Having knocked the wheels off his wagon, Megan leaned back against the wall.

Gray Wolf's face turned nearly as red as Megan's. "You discovered all that?"

She nodded. "I did."

"You're certain that she is not a Comanche?"

"Absolutely."

"You can't know that she was a captive."

Megan held up one finger. "She was white. Despite what TV and the movies may say, the Comanches didn't ask strangers to live with them and certainly not Texans of any age, sex, or color. They seldom even invited a visitor into their tipis. If a white person lived with the Comanches, that person was either a captive or adopted by the People."

"I think you are speculating, Dr. Clark. For example, how do you know the woman was a Texan?"

Megan stepped away from the wall and began to pace along the very narrow path from the wall behind Jerry's desk to the door and back again. Her hands were in almost constant motion. She can't tell a story without talking with her hands. "Because from the 1830s and 1840s until the last of the Comanches voluntarily surrendered in 1875, the most brutal raids, the raids which took the most white captives were the raids into Texas. The percentages say she was a Texan. She was also someone's wife, and I say that not only because she was pregnant—she could have been raped at the time of capture—but because she was so loved by a Comanche warrior that he cut off his braids and buried them with her. An unusual practice for a Comanche warrior, as I'm sure Dr. Stevens will agree. I doubt that a warrior would leave a woman so beloved as a slave. Her murder also indicates that she was a white captive, because the People hardly ever spilled one another's blood. Not that they never killed one another, but it was very rare. But someone couldn't forget she wasn't a Comanche by blood, only by adoption. Still, being married to a Comanche, which automatically meant she was adopted into the tribe, should have protected her. Someone hated her very much, so much that the murderer picked up a stone and hit her in the back of the skull. I know because I found a chip of sandstone inside her skull."

She walked over to the window and looked out for a moment. I don't know what she was looking for. When she turned around, she had tears in her eyes. "We'll never know if she had adapted to life as a member of the Nermernuh or was unhappy. We'll never know what date she was captured. She was between twenty and twenty-five when she died. We'll never know how old she was when she was captured. We'll never know where she was living when she was captured except that it was most likely on the Texas frontier. We'll never know if she left a husband dead and scalped when she was taken from her home. We'll never know if her children were captured with her and killed on the trail, or if they were left at home. And she'd had at least one child before becoming pregnant again. The autopsy proves it. We'll never know her name. But the greatest mystery of all is we'll never know who killed her and why."

In the room's silence Megan laid her report on Jerry's desk and walked out the door. I followed her.

The Time and Again Bookstore was located in a brilliantly white stucco building built in the shape of an L. The store logo, a gigantic grandfather clock, was painted on the blank wall of the storefront. Inside, the air smelled of cinnamon and spice. Agnes loved all kinds of fragrances from lilac to magnolia, apple blossom to vanilla. Not for her the musty smell of old paper that brought on a sneezing fit in one out of every two people. Another difference between Agnes' bookstore and the average store is track lighting, so the shop is light with a feeling of space. To the right of the front door was a three-sided checkout counter; to the left was a comfortable seating area with a couch, two easy chairs, plus enough folding chairs for seating for twelve, all arranged in a circle for easy conversation. Beyond the seating area were row after row of tall shelves, with the subject headings painted on polished boards in the shape of grandfather clocks and hanging from the end of each row. There were three-step footstools in each aisle so customers could always reach the highest shelf. The rare books, mostly mysteries, Westerns, and science fiction, lay face out on slanted shelves located just behind the checkout counter so Agnes could keep an eye on them. Some of the books were very expensive, first editions of Agatha Christie for example, while other titles were more reasonable, but none were economical, even those from the 30s, 40s, and 50s by unknown authors. Each title was in a Ziploc plastic bag with a typed label showing author, title, publisher, publishing history, and price. I walked over and looked down the shelves quickly to see what first editions of Westerns there were while Megan hugged Agnes. There was a first edition of Loren Estleman's first Western, *Aces and Eights,* a well-written story of Wild Bill Hickok. I already owned one signed by the author that I picked up at the Western Writers of America Convention the year it was held in Santa Fe. That was either 1981 or 1982, I don't remember which.

"Ryan, it's time to get started," called Megan.

I wandered over and sat on the couch by Megan. That's my one stipulation for joining Murder by the Yard Reading Circle: I always get to sit on the couch. I can wedge myself in the corner, bend my head over an open copy of whatever mystery we're discussing, and I can close my eyes and doze until time to have refreshments, always cookies baked by either Rosemary or Lorene. Rosemary's molasses lace cookies will melt in your mouth, while Lorene's gumdrop cookies nearly provoke a fight to see who gets the last one.

Candi Hobbs cleared her throat. Candi always clears her throat before she speaks. She's a candidate for an antihistamine. "Megan, I think we ought to read an Indian mystery, one by Tony Hillerman for instance, or James D. Doss or Margaret Coel, and the next week read a book by Kathy Reich or Patricia Cornwell or Aaron Elkins. We'd be reading about Indians and anthropologists slash medical examiners to tie in with your discovering the skeleton and the mummy."

Randel patted Candi's thigh. They had been a couple for the last six months or so and were still in the touchy-feely stage. I will give Candi credit for tugging Randel into place like an unmade bed. He looks much better these days since she persuaded him to trim his goatee and wear socks. Wearing socks doesn't sound like it would make a difference, does it? It is since he wore oxfords, not deck shoes. Candi will have Randel looking presentable in another decade.

"I second Candi's idea," said Randel. "It's time we read something with a background in science or the social sciences. I nominate *Curses!* by Aaron Elkins for next week, followed by *A Thief of Time* by Tony Hillerman."

I didn't think Candi's idea was worth a damn. In fact, I thought it was the worst idea I ever heard. Those kinds of books will only encourage Megan to do a little amateur sleuthing. Where Megan is concerned, mysteries ought to be labeled like cigarettes: dangerous to your health.

Rosemary clapped her hands. "Wonderful choices, Randal. I just love Gideon Oliver. He's such a brilliant physical anthropologist. And it's so nice that Jim Chee and Joe Leaphorn finally met, don't you think, Herb? One would think, though, that they would have met before since the Navajo Reservation doesn't have that large a population." She looked at me. "The Navajo Reservation doesn't have a large population, does it, Ryan?"

I coughed, trying to cover my confusion. I was still trying to figure out who Gideon Oliver was and if Megan might know him and if he would warn her about interfering with a police investigation. "No, I don't think it does, Rosemary. But the two gentlemen—Navajo aren't they?—should have run across one another. There are rituals that everyone attends. And there aren't that many towns. They should cross paths in one or the other town." I sat back and gradually relaxed, glad I had answered Rosemary's question without making a fool out of myself. I wondered why she and Lorene were staring at me.

"It does cover such a large area, Rosemary. If Jim Chee is on one side of the reservation, and Joe Leaphorn is on the other side, then they might keep missing each other," said Lorene. "But Jim Chee *had* heard of Joe Leaphorn, hadn't he? I mean, Joe Leaphorn is such a famous man." She looked at me. "What do you think, Ryan? Is it logical to believe that they could keep missing one another for several years?"

Who are these two guys? I visit my friends on the Navajo Reservation every year, and I never heard of Jim Leaphorn and Joe Chee. If this Leaphorn was that famous, I should have at least heard the name. "What was your question, Lorene? I was trying to remember if I assigned my frontier-life class the outside reading I wanted to discuss with them tomorrow. Sometimes I think my mind is going."

Lorene reached over and patted my knee. "You're too young to worry about being forgetful, Ryan. But my question was do you think it's logical to believe that Chee and Leaphorn kept missing each other for several years?

"I think so. After all, I'm not familiar with either name, and I visit the reservation regularly." Everyone looked puzzled.

Megan hit me in the ribs with her elbow. "Don't answer anymore questions." Her voice sounded like the hiss of a snake. To avoid being bitten, I didn't say anything else.

Herb coughed, another affectation—or maybe the sign of a shy man trying to catch everyone's attention. "Perhaps we can learn something from both books that will help the police investigation."

"That's an excellent idea, Herb," said Agnes. "Megan, you promised to tell us everything you discovered about the skeleton and mummy. Does everyone have notebooks or paper for notes? Megan, you have the floor."

I was horrified to see that everyone had a nice, new note-book and a Bic pen, including Lieutenant Roberts. "Just a minute," I began.

Megan scooted to the edge of the couch. "In the first place, the mummy wasn't a Comanche."

native

9

What the mind doesn't know, the eyes don't cry over.

—Johnny Aysgarth in Francis Iles's
Before the Fact, 1932

PALO DURO CANYON, 1868

"I'll go talk to Buffalo Woman," Spotted Tongue told Green Willow. "Perhaps she saw something or heard something that will lead me to the murderer."

Green Willow sat on her trade blanket in her arbor, pushing a bone awl through the buckskin that she planned as a dress. When there were sufficient holes in the buckskin, she would thread the buffalo sinew through them and tie off the sinew when she reached the end of the seam. It was hard work and time consuming, but Spotted Tongue knew Green Willow enjoyed sitting in the arbor listening to the other women talking, and the warriors bragging about what they had done on the last raid, and what they planned to do on the next one. Her hands were busy but her spirit was calm.

Green Willow laid down her bone awl and considered Spotted Tongue's statement. "Yes, I think Buffalo Woman will have something to say. She always has something to say, but whether she's enlightening is another matter."

"She has as many winters as you but she hasn't married. I wonder why."

"Oh, Spotted Tongue, you know so little about women. She's waiting for you to take her as your second wife. That is why she always sets up her tipi next to yours. Her parents are old and ill, and she has no brothers to hunt for her. If you didn't take her buffalo meat and other game, she and her parents would have to depend on what she can kill. She is a good hunter, but she must watch over her parents and tend to all the other things that must be done, so she depends on your help or the family would go hungry much of the time. She needs a husband and she wants you."

Spotted Tongue was astonished. He had fallen into the habit of providing for Buffalo Woman and her parents, but he didn't offer ponies for her. Perhaps if he hadn't captured Little Flower, he might have eventually taken Buffalo Woman for his second wife. She was a good worker and might carry a child as Green Willow hadn't. But Little Flower took all his heart and he gave it willingly. She brought him joy with her eyes the deep blue color of the sky when evening comes, and her soft black hair that curled around his fingers. He swallowed, trying to soothe the pain of unshed tears caught in his throat. He would have blood for blood from whoever took his woman despite the fact that it wasn't the Nermernuh way. He must have relief from the sickness of grief.

"How would you feel if I took Buffalo Woman for my second wife?" he asked Green Willow, curious about how two wives of the Nermernuh would get along. Would Buffalo Woman and Green Willow, both Nerms, be like sisters or not? As long as wives didn't bother a warrior's peace, men of the Nermernuh didn't care how much the women might fight among themselves. And if one wife made trouble, most men would beat the troublemaking out of her or send her back to her parents. Spotted Tongue knew most men wouldn't bother to puzzle over how women think. He didn't know why he did except that Little Flower changed him.

Green Willow shrugged her shoulders. "She's a good worker and could help look after our children if I ever quicken. I wouldn't object. She'll never take your heart away from me, because you no longer have it to give her. You buried it with Little Flower. Buffalo Woman will be company for me. At least she speaks our tongue."

"Little Flower would have had a child when the first snows fell," he said, then tightened his lips so that his chin wouldn't tremble. Warriors didn't cry.

Green Willow's head snapped up in shock. "I didn't know. She held her secret well. I am so sorry for all of us. This tipi needs the sound of a child's laughter. I would have called her sister and welcomed her child." She laid down her sewing. "Spotted Tongue, find her murderer for he has murdered our children. I want to wash my hands in his blood."

"I'll go talk to Buffalo Woman," he said and escaped from her presence. He couldn't handle her woman's grief and anger in addition to his own.

He saw Buffalo Woman sitting in her arbor with her parents. Her father's face was wrinkled like an apple dried in the sun, and his fingers were twisted until he could not hold a bow or lance. He had only a few teeth left in his mouth, and he walked with the help of a stick. His back was bowed and his eyes were covered with a dull coating. He saw only shadows and then only in bright sunlight. Buffalo Woman's mother saw only darkness with both her eyes and her mind. Spotted Tongue feared her parents because he saw himself in them in only a handful of winters. A Nerm's life was short and too often full of suffering.

He stood outside Buffalo Woman's arbor and called her name as was polite.

She rose to invite him in. "Spotted Tongue, I'm sorry that your second wife died. I know you grieve for her."

"She didn't die, she was murdered." Each time he said the word "murdered," his bitterness and rage increased.

"Who is here, daughter?" asked Buffalo Woman's father as he tried to tilt his head back to peer in the direction of the visitor's voice. His back was so bowed that his head almost sank between his shoulders like a tortoise pulling his head into his shell.

"It's Spotted Tongue, Father."

Buffalo Woman's father cupped his hand around his ear. "Did he say his second wife was murdered?"

"Yes, Father, and please don't interrupt anymore," said Buffalo Woman, sounding as if she was at the end of her patience.

"Murdered!" her father exclaimed, shaking his head. "That isn't the way of the Nermernuh, young Spotted Tongue. We didn't murder one another in my day. But these young warriors today think only of blood and war. If they don't make war every full moon, then they fight each other. It's bad. It's very bad." He shook a twisted finger in the air. "Hear what I say, you young ones! It's the curse of the Cannibal Owl. It eats the goodness of the Nermernuh as if eating mice from the prairie and leaves only the bad spirits that want more slaves, more wives, more of the white man's goods, more ponies! More, more, more! Soon the Nermernuh will be no better than the Tejanos. It didn't used to be that way." The old man's mouth worked as if his words left a bad taste in his mouth.

"Yes, Father, now hush so I can talk to Spotted Tongue," said Buffalo Woman, stepping closer to Spotted Tongue and lowering her voice. "I'm sorry he complained of how these days are so bad compared to his youth. He talks about the past until I have to leave. He talks about we younger ones as if we haven't done anything good for the Nermernuh." She touched her hair which she wore a little longer than Green

Willow. "Now, what did you want to talk about with me?"

Spotted Tongue wished he hadn't listened to the old man. There was enough truth in his words to chill the young warrior's heart. He forced himself to answer Buffalo Woman. "You and Slow Like a Turtle were picking plums with Little Flower after Green Willow came back to camp. Who else was there?"

"Wild Horse's wife, Deer Fawn, who will meet her child when the moon turns full again. She's frightened and cries over nothing the closer her time comes, so the rest of us women don't tell her of Wild Horse sneaking around to teach your second wife how to shoot a bow and arrow. She didn't like Little Flower anyway, and we were worried that if she found out about Wild Horse, well, the news might bring on the baby too soon."

Spotted Tongue felt as if he had swallowed a hot stone. One of his closest friends was teaching Little Flower. That wasn't Wild Horse's place, but Spotted Tongue didn't intend to reveal his anger to Buffalo Woman. Women gossiped too much. Word of his friend's perfidy would race through the camp faster than his white mare fleeing the Tejanos after a raid.

"What's there to find out about Wild Horse and Little Flower? He is teaching her a skill she needs. What's wrong with that?" asked Spotted Tongue.

Buffalo Woman shrugged her shoulders. "I don't know of anything going on that shouldn't, and I wouldn't accuse Little Flower of doing anything improper, but why did they keep her lessons secret? That made me suspicious. Doesn't it make you wonder, too, Spotted Tongue?"

"Who else was there, Buffalo Woman?" asked Spotted Tongue, promising himself to deal with Wild Horse's betrayal later.

She tapped her cheek with one finger as she thought. She

perfidy - deceitfulness

tilted her head and smiled. "Shaking Hand's wife was there. What is her name? I can't remember right now." Her tone of voice said she didn't care if she remembered or not.

"Topay," said Spotted Tongue.

Buffalo Woman smiled at him. "That's right, Topay. Anyway, she was giving Little Flower black looks and telling the rest of us that she would leave Shaking Hand's tipi and return to her parents if he didn't stop going off alone with her. He tells her that he's teaching Little Flower our tongue, but Topay doesn't believe him. And who knows what a man will get up to when he's alone in the bushes with a woman?"

Spotted Tongue felt nauseated at the thought of his friends and Little Flower. It wasn't the custom to offer such kindnesses to a white captive not your own. Indeed, it wasn't the custom to offer kindnesses to any white captive unless it's a child you have adopted. Nor did white captives try to make friends with their captors, at least, no one with as many winters as Little Flower. He felt sick with grief thinking of his friends and what they may have really been doing with Little Flower. He glanced at the avid expression on Buffalo Woman's face and remembered why he had never offered horses for her. She relished gossip too much and repeated it too often. She would bring trouble to his tipi.

"I'm sure that Shaking Hands is telling his wife the truth. I trust my friends." He nearly gagged on his words.

Buffalo Woman laid her hand on his bare chest. "Spotted Tongue, give up your grief. She is happier beyond the sun than she was with the People. She wasn't happy as either your wife or a Nerm. I saw her so many times standing by herself and crying. But you didn't see her unhappiness because you didn't want to see it."

"Do you know who the last women to leave were?" he asked, ignoring Buffalo Woman's judgements even though they made him angry. It was no wonder that her father had

never been offered horses for her. No one wanted a bossy woman.

Buffalo Woman turned away and looked toward the little canyon. "Myself and Slow Like a Turtle. I didn't see anyone else, but the walls of that little canyon are not as steep as the walls in the big canyon. Someone could have climbed down after we left. But not Wild Horse's wife. She's entirely too big and clumsy."

Spotted Tongue nodded his head several times. "Yes, well, thank you, Buffalo Woman. I have a place to start looking for Little Flower's murderer."

Spotted Tongue stood outside Buffalo Woman's arbor, thinking of what to do next. He walked over to join his friends and squatted down on his heels by Fat Belly. His friend was gambling with Shaking Hand and Wild Horse. Shaking Hand had as many arrows as he had fingers and toes. Wild Horse and Fat Belly each had only a few arrows remaining for Shaking Hand to win. They were rolling the tiny square boxes with spots on each side that the Comancheros called dice. They would bet that they could call the number of dots that appeared on the top side of the square when they rolled the dice. Spotted Horse would bet on horse races, on how many buffalo he could kill in an hour, whether he was the best at shooting with the bow and arrow, or on how far he could throw the lance. He would never bet on the dice, especially not now that he couldn't make medicine, because he couldn't influence the outcome. Shaking Hand must have made powerful medicine to win so often at dice.

Shaking Hand won again and took another arrow from Fat Belly and Wild Horse. He glanced at Spotted Tongue's lack of braids, but out of politeness said nothing. "I hurt for you, Spotted Tongue. She was a beautiful woman and very smart. We'll all miss her."

"I'm sure you'll miss her. How much will you miss my wife?" Spotted Tongue grabbed his friend's hand and began forcing his thumb toward his wrist. "Did you teach my wife anything besides words? Did you murder her when you tired of her, so I wouldn't find out and demand compensation for your use of her? Or did you murder her so she would be gone, and your wife would stop threatening to leave your tipi and return to her parents? Did you make a cuckold of me and a fool out of your wife?"

Wild Horse and Fat Belly scrambled over to the two men and pulled Spotted Tongue away from Shaking Hand. "Spotted Tongue, how can you be witless enough to accuse your friend of adultery? Hold his arms tight, Wild Horse. Let's drop him in the stream to cool him off."

"I'll demand that he give me ten ponies for the injury he did my honor, not to mention my hand," said Shaking Hand, following Fat Belly and Wild Horse as they carried Spotted Tongue to the stream. "My thumb is swelling and my hand will be useless for many days. I won't be able to hunt because I can't hold a bow. I'll hope that the Tejanos won't ride through our camp because I won't be much good at defending my wife and child."

Wild Horse and Fat Belly dropped Spotted Tongue into the stream. Every time he tried to crawl upon the bank, the other two warriors would push him back. "Have you found your wits, Spotted Tongue? Did the little men steal them? Or do you believe the tales that old women tell?" asked Wild Horse.

"Enough!" cried Spotted Tongue. He sat on the stream's bottom with only his head and shoulders above water. Exhaustion weighed down his body and shame weighed down his heart. He wished he could blame the little men, those mischievous little beings who hid from the People, but he couldn't. His behavior was his own fault.

Spotted Tongue crawled out of the stream and rested his hand on his friend's shoulder. "Shaking Hand, I'll bring you ten ponies tomorrow, ten ponies from among the best I have. It won't take away my shame or heal your hurt, but maybe it'll repay you for the insult to your honor. I'm crazy with grief for Little Flower and cannot think any but crazy thoughts. I'll be crazy until I take revenge for her murder."

The four friends sat on the bank of the stream and dangled their feet in the water. "Who would do such a thing?" asked Wild Horse. "It's bad medicine and against our customs. Who would risk your anger by taking your wife away from you? It's known that you don't forgive an injury, and that you are skilled with both the bow and the knife."

"It's not just my wife I grieve for, Wild Horse. Little Flower would have had my child in four more moons. Two lives were murdered." He bowed his head to hide his wet eyes from the other warriors.

Spotted Tongue's friends didn't speak for many minutes as they pondered what Spotted Tongue had told them. That someone would kill one of the People, and one who was pregnant by a respected warrior appalled them. It would be a different matter if Little Flower had already been pregnant when she was captured. "It wasn't me," said Wild Horse finally. "I was teaching her to use the bow and arrow. She was strong and could shoot an arrow nearly as far as I can. I'll break the bow I made her over her grave that she'll have it in the land beyond the sun."

"Why did you teach her, Wild Horse? Would you let another warrior so close to your wife? Was your behavior honorable? Or did you make a cuckold out of me?"

"Spotted Tongue, my friend, calm yourself. Your second wife, Little Flower, would always keep her distance. She wouldn't allow me close enough to touch her in an improper way. She was your woman. Did you never see her *watching you? If someone wanted to make a cuckold of you with Little Flower, he would have to rape her. She would never willingly surrender to any man but you."*

Spotted Tongue felt dizzy from lack of sleep and anger and couldn't think. But his head was clear enough to disregard Wild Horse's words. Little Flower didn't love him. He would have known if she had. And he shouldn't have confronted his friends. He was too tired to separate truth from lies. He must be clever like the fox and attack them when they weren't looking. If he discovered one of his friends was lying, he would have revenge. There was a taboo against one Nerm killing another, but if murder happened, as it had to Little Flower, then he had a right to kill the murderer without retribution being taken by the victim's family. And the taboo had been broken more frequently lately, so he might as well disregard it, too.

He leaned over and splashed water on his face over and over again. When he felt that he had control over his tongue, he staggered up. "Fat Belly, my first wife said that some of the women stayed behind with Little Flower. Your wife, Slow Like a Turtle, was one of the women. I would like to question her about what she remembers, but I didn't want to do it without telling you first."

Fat Belly waved his hand in the direction of his arbor. "Go talk to her. Maybe she'll tell you something that you need to know. On the other hand, maybe she won't. Maybe she'll give you a kiss or maybe she'll empty a pot of boiled buffalo over your head. Never know from day to day what that woman will do. That's why I spend so much time around the fire with Shaking Hand and Wild Horse. I always know what they'll do. Shaking Hand will always win when we gamble, and Wild Horse will lose as much as I do." Fat Belly slapped Spotted Tongue's back. "You're a good friend, Spotted Tongue, just a little crazy is all. If you had eaten some *buffalo meat this morning like I told you to, and slept in your arbor and let your wits recover, you would be better off now."*

"Food isn't the answer for every hurt, Fat Belly," said Spotted Tongue.

Fat Belly's eyes widened and his mouth dropped open. "It isn't? I didn't know that. I thought it was. Buffalo meat has always comforted me. It makes everything feel better. That's why I laugh all day. I eat buffalo all the time."

Spotted Tongue didn't know if Fat Belly was serious or not, and he was too tired to figure it out.

not Ryan

10

Though a man may sometimes escape the public consequences of his acts, he cannot escape his own character.

—Belief of Sir Evelyn,
Reputation for a Song, 1952

AMARILLO, TEXAS, PRESENT DAY

Megan sat in Jerry Carr's office the day after her introduction to Gray Wolf Murphy. "Can you believe that phony Comanche and his shaman act?"

"Now, Megan, we don't know that he's a phony," said Ryan.

"How many Comanches do you know with blond hair, blue eyes, and pale skin? I bet he goes through as much sunscreen in a day as I do."

"I don't know any Comanches with blond hair," said Ryan. "Of course, I don't know many Comanches, but with several decades of intermarriage between whites and Comanches, anything is possible, even a blond shaman."

"I still think he's a phony. There's a mystery writer named Sharyn McCrumb who believes that in America we can pick our ethnic background. Do you want to be a Scot? Buy yourself a kilt, some kneesocks, a long scarf to throw over your shoulder, a kirk, and voilá, you're from the land of Mary, Queen of Scots. Works for all the other ethnic groups: same ploy, different props. Mr. Gray Wolf Murphy may have an eyedropper full of Comanche blood, but give him a feathered headdress, knee-high moccasins, braided hair, and voilá, he's a shaman."

"That's not quite right," interrupted Ryan. "Feathered headdresses are not truly Comanche. When the Comanches and the Kiowas became allies instead of enemies, the Comanches picked up the idea of feathered headdresses from the Kiowas. Then, of course, the Eastern press expected all Plains Horse Indians to look alike, which they did not until reservation life and eastern expectations homogenized them. The original headdress which the Comanches wore when they went to war or on a raid, was the hide of a buffalo head, horns and all. Their war paint was black and white horizontal stripes across the face. Those Europeans, mainly the Spanish colonists in Texas and New Mexico, and the early explorers and military men from what is now the United States, say that the Comanches were the most frightening-looking horse Indians of all."

"Ryan," began Megan.

He got up, making gestures with his hands and totally ignoring Megan. "Imagine! You're a Spanish colonist on the eastern edge of New Mexico in about 1750, and suddenly, as if they rose out of the ground, comes riding out of a rising full moon, nearly naked men riding like satyrs, wearing buffalo-hide headdresses, black and white war paint, and carrying quivers full of arrows and fourteen-foot lances. In the moonlight the warriors look as if they have horns. The colonists believe they are seeing devils! Their Pueblo Indian servants whisper that dreaded word 'Comanche' and being very intelligent, run like hell as far and as fast as they can, calling upon the icons of both their native religion and Christianity—just to cover all their bases!

The Comanches were magnificent! They were a warrior culture, one of the last, undefeated until vastly outnumbered by an army led by a colonel who understood that to win a war against the Comanche it was necessary to destroy their horses. Because, you see—"

Megan interrupted in a loud voice. "We get the picture, Ryan! As I was saying, Jerry, culture is learned, not inherited. I would be embarrassed to pretend to be something I'm not, but apparently that doesn't bother our shaman. I repeat, Gray Wolf Murphy is a phony."

"He may also be a murderer," said Jerry Carr soberly. "We took the results of your examination of the skeleton and started five years back looking for a missing person. We found five, but only one fit your criteria. Right age, right height, right sex. We located her dentist to verify your work, and in your words, voilá, we have a name for our skeleton: Mrs. Jessica Murphy, wife of Mr. Gray Wolf Murphy. And guess what? The Murphys—or rather, Mr. Murphy—lives on the rim of the canyon, just above where her body was buried."

"What does Gray Wolf Murphy say about this coincidence?" asked Megan.

"What do you think? He's innocent. Do you think he would admit it if he wasn't?"

"This is very interesting," said Megan in a thoughtful tone of voice.

Jerry Carr sat straight up in his chair, an earnest, but uneasy expression on his face. "I shared this information with you because, frankly, we would still be hunting down dentists to identify our skeleton if you hadn't done a very competent job examining Jessica Murphy's bones. You helped a lot, Megan. Without you, Jessica Murphy would still be Jane Doe."

Megan smiled and curtsied. She thought about saying

"I told you so," but decided that would be stretching Jerry's gratitude, which, judging by the expression on his face, was already stretched to the snapping point. "Maybe next time I tell you I can help, you'll believe me. So what else can I do?"

The lieutenant rubbed his left eye which had suddenly developed a tic on the lower lid. "The answer is nothing. Special Crimes can handle the investigation from here on. I'll arrange for Randall County to pay you for your work if you will submit a bill."

"This is kind of a sudden dismissal," said Megan with a disappointed expression.

The lieutenant walked around his desk to sit on its edge by Megan's chair. "You must have been expecting it, Megan. We've had this argument before. You're not a peace officer, you're a civilian. If you interfere with this investigation, I will charge you with interference with public duties, so help me God. You're not Miss Marple, and this is not a mystery story."

"Jerry, if the members of Murder by the Yard Reading Circle hadn't stepped in, I know of three cases that would still be unsolved because you were looking in entirely the wrong direction at entirely the wrong person."

The lieutenant returned to his chair and sat down. "I don't deny that you and your gang of amateur sleuths have given Special Crimes some accurate tips—"

Megan leapt out of her chair. "Tips are what you call in over the phone or whisper in a detective's ear in some smoky bar. And we don't interfere with public duties. We just assure that the focus of those public duties isn't blurry. Come on, Ryan. It's obvious we are accomplishing nothing here." She swept out the door like an offended rock star whose last album got a bad review in *Rolling Stone*.

"Oh, I think we're accomplishing a lot," said Ryan in a whisper to Jerry Carr. "Megan just created a predicament."

Megan peeled out of the parking lot in her extended-cab GMC, gratified that her tinkering with the truck's engine added a spark to its performance. That was the only thing she found that was gratifying this morning. And the victim's name. She wondered if Gray Wolf Murphy did kill his wife. She hoped not; it was too easy. She liked her cases complicated. Not that this was her case. She had no unofficial client to seek justice for like she'd had in her other cases, and she thought she might be testing Jerry's patience to dive into an investigation in which she had no personal interest. Yes, Jerry had sounded very serious this morning, and she wasn't really interested in going to jail. There was such a low class of people in jail, and the accommodations smelled of urine and Lysol. She knew this not from experience, but from a personal tour with her own police officer as a guide. She thought at the time that Jerry Carr had an ulterior motive in showing her the facilities.

She glanced at Ryan twisted around in his seat as usual. The next truck she bought would have bucket seats, so Ryan would have enough leg room. She turned south on Ong Street where she and Ryan lived. Speaking of whom, why wasn't he talking? "Ryan, why are you so quiet? You haven't said a word since we left Jerry's office."

"I'm psyching myself up for the predicament," he said with his eyes closed.

"What predicament are you talking about? Are you having problems with your classes?"

"My classes are fine; it's my extracurricular activities that worry me."

Puzzled as to what extracurricular activities he was referring to, she pulled her truck into her driveway and parked. She turned in her seat to ask him to explain himself when she heard the sound of a car door slamming shut. She looked in her rearview mirror and saw a familiar-looking man walking up her driveway. She nudged Ryan. "Open your eyes and tell me if that man walking up my driveway is Gray Wolf Murphy."

Ryan blinked a few times and looked out Megan's rear window. "That looks like the shaman himself. I wonder what he wants."

Megan slid out of her truck, feeling the excitement grow. "Mr. Murphy, what can I do for you today?"

Gray Wolf Murphy gave the impression of a balloon with the air leaking out. He seemed to have shrunk since she met him twenty-four hours ago. "Dr. Clark, I've read about you in the newspaper before yesterday. You have a reputation of sorts for solving crimes"—he stopped to draw breath—"and I seem to be involved in one. A crime I mean."

Megan unlocked her front door to be greeted by Rembrandt and Horatio, both of them chastising her for deserting them and assuring her that they would forgive her for the price of a dog treat. "You boys don't jump on my guest. In fact, why don't I let you go play in the backyard." They looked at her as if she had proposed buying a cat to come live in their house. No animal, including humans, could look so betrayed as a dog. They followed her to the back door with their tales between their legs.

She returned to the living room to find Gray Wolf Murphy standing in her open front door nervously trying to decide whether to come in or go out. He didn't know it but she would tackle him if he tried to get away. "Come in, Mr. Murphy. I don't want to discuss your personal distress in public. It is bad enough to be involved in a crime without the whole world, or at least Amarillo, Texas, knowing about it." She turned to make sure Ryan had followed the shaman. He had, looking as worried as if he was responsible for the state of the world. "Ryan, would you call Herb? Mr. Murphy will need a lawyer."

Gray Wolf looked confused and frightened. "Why do I need a lawyer? I haven't done anything."

"That's why you need a lawyer. The guilty usually have such a criminal track record that they could quote the courtroom legalese well enough to fool the average person. And they know not to say a word except to ask for a Coke and to go to the bathroom. It's the innocent who talk too much and find their words twisted until they wonder if they are guilty after all." She looked him straight in the eye. "You are innocent, aren't you, Mr. Murphy?"

"Yes, I've never committed a crime in my life," he said with the earnest expression of the naïve. "But you don't know what I'm accused of."

"You haven't been accused of anything yet, or you would be in jail waiting to be charged. But I know what you will be accused of if Special Crimes can dredge up enough evidence for a grand jury to indict you. Jerry Carr and Special Crimes believe that you stabbed your wife to death."

Gray Wolf looked as if he might collapse. "But, Dr. Clark—"

"No! Don't tell me anything about your wife's disappearance, your marriage, hobbies, pets, aspirations, anything until the lawyer gets here, because if the district attorney subpoenas me to appear against you, I will have to repeat anything you tell me. Anything you tell me is not privileged information because I'm not a lawyer or a priest, two professions to whom you can confess that you keep little children locked in a closet, and they can't repeat it. So let's talk about some innocuous subject until Herb arrives. Do you think we'll have an early snow this winter?"

Gray Wolf looked puzzled and even more confused as if he couldn't figure out why she suddenly started talking about the weather. "I don't like snow," he finally said.

Ryan slipped into the living room and sat down on the couch by Megan. He looked resigned and she wondered to what. She reached over and squeezed his hand, then kept holding it to assure him that she was there if he needed her. He raised one eyebrow, an example of physical dexterity she had never been able to duplicate.

The doorbell rang. Herbert Jackson III, attorney at law, had arrived. "Mr. Murphy, if you would pay me a dollar so legally I represent you, we'll discuss my fee after I hear your story and decide if I will represent you any longer than this afternoon," said Herb, setting his briefcase on the coffee table and removing a receipt book, a yellow legal pad, and two pens. "I will hire Dr. Clark and Dr. Stevens for a dollar apiece, so they can work as my legal assistants and not be subject to subpoena by the district attorney. They can question witnesses and look at evidence, and Lieutenant Jerry Carr can't arrest them for interference with public duties. They aren't private investigators, but working for me they don't have to be. Any notes they take will be legally work-related, and the district attorney can't subpoena them either. Now, Mr. Murphy, please tell us your story of your wife's disappearance. Begin with the last day you saw her and continue to the present."

Murphy rested his elbows on his thighs and rubbed his hands together. "I didn't know if Jessica had disappeared or had deserted me. We had been arguing off and on for months because I was gone so much fulfilling my obligations as a shaman, so it wasn't impossible to think that she had deserted me. I finally had sense enough to check her belongings to see if anything was gone. Well, there were no clothes missing that I could tell, and her toothbrush and prescription drugs were in the medicine cabinet, so I decided she had disappeared. I called the police to report her missing."

"When was this?" asked Megan, studying his demeanor. He looked nervous and scared.

Murphy thought a moment. "I reported her missing on September twenty-fourth, five years ago. I had been in Oklahoma for ten days and got home on September twenty-third. I waited a day before I called the police because I thought she might be out with friends and decided to spend the night. The police came out on September twenty-fifth and grilled me pretty good. I know they questioned some of her friends because they told me later, but I didn't think they worked very hard hunting for her. The detective who was investigating—I don't remember his name—told me that most adults who go missing mean to be missing. They disappear because they want to. I told him that I didn't think she would leave all her clothes if she was taking off forever. And I really worried about her prescription drugs. She had high blood pressure and high cholesterol and Type I diabetes—all of those disorders were hereditary—or rather the predisposition to develop those disorders is hereditary. But if you have all three of those disorders, and you don't stay on your medication, then you're just a heart attack or stroke waiting to happen, and Jessica knew that. No way would she have left those drugs. The doctor told her that the drugs were the only thing standing between her and death. I tried to tell the detective that, but I don't think I ever got through to him that somebody took her out of that house against her will, because her car was still there. Or maybe somebody forced her into his car if she was out walking. She tried to exercise every day. Had to, really. She stayed thin because weight aggravates those three disorders, and she needed lots of exercise to maintain her weight. Diabetics tend to gain weight easily and that's dangerous. So that's the story," he said, rubbing his hands over his face. He looked paler than he had yesterday.

Gray Wolf looked out the living room window as though his wife might come walking up the sidewalk to the front door. Finally, he caught his breath as if he had forgotten to breathe for a time and continued talking. "For a long time I thought her body would show up, but there are a lot of places you can hide a body in this country. Then I thought maybe she'd call me out of the blue. For a couple of years I'd jump every time the phone rang because I thought it might be her. It never was, of course, and thinking back on it, I decided I must have been a little crazy for a year or more. Then I quit expecting her to call or to show up. I knew she was dead, had to be, but I didn't have a body to bury. Ever since I've given up hope she's alive, I've just been waiting for seven years to pass so I can have her declared legally dead and go on with my life."

"Who did the police question?" asked Megan.

Gray Wolf rubbed his chin. "The ladies in her bridge club, our neighbors. She was a volunteer at the museum, so the detective talked to Dr. Norman Ryland. I guess that's all. Everybody said she was a nice woman, and nobody could think of a reason for me to kill her, so the case kind of petered out. And that's my story."

Herb stood and shook hands with Gray Wolf, told him to stop by the office to talk about Herb's fee, and told him under no circumstances to talk to the police or to the press. Megan watched Gray Wolf drive off and started to pace.

Ryan stood up and stepped in front of her. He clasped her shoulders to hold her still. "Just a minute, Megan. What was all that about, having Herb drive over here so Gray Wolf could hire him? And us? Investigators? I thought you had our neighborhood shaman at the top of your suspect list. You called him a phony. What is your devious brain thinking of now?"

"I am not devious! Sometimes I just skip over steps in

my thought processes. Sometimes that confuses people."
She gave him a deliberate stare to let him know he was one
of those confused and lifted his hands off her shoulders. "I
still think Gray Wolf Murphy is a phony, but I don't think
he's a murderous phony. Do you agree?"

"I felt sorry for him," said Ryan. "I would hate to sit in
my house for five years and not know where my wife was.
And I don't think he killed his wife. I didn't hear any hate
when he talked about her. But that's beside the point. I'm
not the one doing the 180-degree turn. I want to know what
changed your mind."

Megan flinched at the expression on his face. Apparently Ryan was going to stand in the middle of her living
room until he grew roots if she didn't enlighten him. "Did
your mother ever have one particular rule that she repeated
at least once a day until even today you find yourself repeating it?

"Not once a day, three times a day. Eat your breakfast—
or lunch—or dinner, Ryan. Think about all the starving
children in Bangladesh. I always wanted to tell her to wrap
up our meal and mail it to Bangladesh, but I figured she'd
send me to my room after telling me little boys who talked
back to their mothers came to a sorry end."

"My mother never told me anything like that."

"Your mother was more interested in providing a meal
so no one could say she neglected you, than actually per-
suading you to eat. The sooner you pushed your plate away,
the sooner she could send you next door to stay with us and
she could go to her committee or hearing or protest with a
clear conscience."

Megan flinched again. Ryan had a way of cutting to the
chase that made her very uncomfortable. She knew her
mother always considered the big picture like nuclear waste

or saving the whales or breast cancer or domestic violence rather than the small snapshot of a little girl who wanted frosted flakes for breakfast sometimes instead of hot oatmeal and a piece of toast. Sometimes her mother forgot the toast.

"My mother did the best she knew how, Ryan. She just didn't know a lot of parenting skills. But she did teach me one thing that has saved us both a lot of trouble. She told me as least ten times a day—when she was home—never to talk to the police without your lawyer present. I was just reacting to my mother's mantra by calling Herb to represent Gray Wolf. I was raised to feel responsible for anyone caught up in the criminal justice system. Besides—"Megan snapped her mouth shut, but it was too late.

"Aha! I knew there was a besides. Cough it up. Megan."

She gritted her teeth. Ryan was beginning to know her too well. "Besides, by working as investigators for Herb while he represents Gray Wolf is a foolproof way to be involved in the case without worrying about Jerry Carr arresting us for interference with a public officer."

Ryan fell back on the couch and looked up at the ceiling. "My God! I knew it! You're playing Agatha Christie again!"

"Agatha Christie is the author, Ryan. Miss Marple is the detective figure, and I'm not Miss Marple. I'm more like Kinsey Millhone."

Ryan covered his face with his hands. "That's what I'm afraid of," he said in a muffled voice. "She killed somebody in her first book."

Megan wished she had mentioned another female sleuth besides Kinsey Millhone. *A Is for Alibi* was the only mystery Ryan had read since college. Well, Ryan would just have to get over it.

"Herb, Ryan and I will start interviewing Gray Wolf's neighbors. Those houses on the rim of Little Sunday Canyon are built really close together. Someone had to have seen or heard something. We'll see if we can find somebody bearing tales."

11

A enemy can partly ruin a man, but it takes a good-natured injudicious friend to complete the thing and make it perfect.

—Mark Twain's *Pudd'nhead Wilson*, 1894

LITTLE SUNDAY CANYON, PRESENT DAY

The temperature was in the low 90s since it was September. A month earlier the temperature had been in the triple digits. The pasture land on each side of the road was its usual dried tan color from the summer heat and lack of rain. The only vegetation still green were the mesquite trees and the yucca and prickly pear cactus. The cacti never turned brown even in the dead of winter. The leaves on the cottonwood, plum, and every other kind of tree in the canyon hadn't started turning yet. I was sorry. The cottonwood always turned the brightest, most beautiful shade of yellow. I liked to walk through a grove of cottonwoods and listen to the wind rustling the leaves. Their music was different in the fall when the leaves turned.

"I think we ought to start with the neighbors on each side of Gray Wolf. What do you think?" asked Megan as she turned left off Washington and headed toward the canyon at a speed just under breakneck. She wore a red T-shirt, a denim skirt, and brown leather flats instead of her usual casual wear: cut-offs, work boots, and a UT rowing-club T-shirt.

I tightened my seat belt just short of cutting off my breath. If Megan wrecked this dented, paint-chipped monster, I wanted to survive. "I think someone has gotten away with murder for five years, Megan. He's a dangerous man. He's not going to risk your fingering him."

"Fingering him. *Fingering* him? Ryan, you need to update your slang. Try watching something besides 1930s' gangster movies. As for your fears that some murderer will jump out of the closet and seize me, I don't intend to try to arrest him. That's not my job. That's what Special Crimes is for, to make arrests."

I tried to say something, but all I could do was to stutter. I stuttered loudly, though, so Megan wouldn't jump in and start talking. I finally got myself under control enough that I could talk. "Megan, your logic is is fallible. If you tell Special Crimes who to arrest, you are just as much of a target as if you tried to make the arrest yourself. Don't you understand? The murderer has escaped notice for five years, but now that the body—skeleton—has been found, he's scared, he's nervous, he'll shoot your lights out if he thinks you suspect him!"

Megan reached over and patted my leg, the part she could reach which happened to be my thigh which immediately started tingling. "Ryan, you are really so sweet. You worry about me all the time, don't you?"

I don't know if I appreciate being described as "so sweet." That's how you describe two-year-old, freckled-face, little boys, or an elderly grandfather. I don't fit into either category. Why can't she exclaim "Oh, Ryan, you're so handsome and wonderful. I could just eat you up." Now that's a description a man can appreciate.

Megan turned onto a graded road that ran through a cattle pasture full of curious cattle with no fear of an automobile. I wasn't apprehensive. We were in Megan's GMC behemoth truck that was the equal of a longhorn steer, a testy one.

Megan stopped in front of a small stone house perched on the edge of the canyon that practically hugged Gray Wolf's home on the north. According to the list of neighbors that Gray Wolf gave her, this was the home of Peggy Otlander, a picture-perfect house. Terra cotta pots filled with white, pink, and red geraniums sat on the tiny front porch. Flower beds filled with rose bushes stretched on either side of the porch to the ends of the house. Those flower beds looked so perfect, they appeared artificial. There was hardly any yard, but what was there was shaded by a purple plum tree, its reddish purple leaves in sharp contrast to the brilliant blue sky. It was a beautiful little home with an eye-popping view of the canyon. I'd sell my house and buy one on the edge of the canyon—if it didn't mean I'd have to leave Megan behind. I wouldn't leave a house where I only had to walk across my front yard to hers for all the beautiful views I needed.

I stretched the kinks out of my back from riding in the GMC, then followed Megan to Mrs. Otlander's door. I decided that Megan's skirt was too short. It was at least three inches above the knee. That length showed entirely too much of a beautiful set of legs.

She looked back at me and frowned. "Wake up, Ryan, you look like you're in a daze."

I blinked several times and settled into my attentive mode. It was a facade that allowed me to daydream during faculty meetings without being caught. I thought it would placate Megan.

She shook her head in disapproval. "Now you look like

you've been hypnotized, but maybe Mrs. Otlander will think you're spellbound by her." She assumed her friendly, neighborhood professional woman expression—Megan took one drama course in college and it went to her head—and rang the doorbell. "Hello, Mrs. Otlander. I'm Dr. Megan Clark and this is Dr. Ryan Stevens. We are working for Mr. Gray Wolf Murphy's attorney, investigating the disappearance and subsequent murder of Jessica Murphy, and we would like to ask some questions and get your impressions of Ms. Murphy."

"Come in here and sit down," she said, holding her door open. Her home was as tidy and orderly inside as outside. Mrs. Otlander matched her home: a neat and tidy woman with a perpetual smile, who reminded me so much of Donna Reed that I was surprised she was wearing slacks instead of a dress and heels. I estimated her to be in her late thirties, maybe a year or two older that Gray Wolf, but still young to be a widow. I wondered what happened to Mr. Otlander.

She served us iced tea and homemade cookies, fussed until we were sitting on the couch, because she declared it was more comfortable than the two chairs in the room. But none of her welcoming sounds as a Donna Reed hostess interfered with her conversation about Gray Wolf and his situation, and demonstrated that she could talk longer on one breath of air than anyone I've listened to in years. Her lung capacity was unbelievable. I wondered how long she could stay underwater before coming up for air.

"That was so terrible, your finding Jessica buried like that, Dr. Clark. To think of all those years that Gray Wolf searched and grieved, and she was buried less that a hundred feet away all the time. I was with him Sunday night when you found Jessica and that mummy. He was excited about the mummy, thinking it was Comanche and all, and I was so happy for him. Then late the next day Lieutenant

Carr drove down to tell Gray Wolf that the skeleton was Jessica. And to question him. I was glad I was there, too, because that man didn't even give Gray Wolf a chance to adjust to the horror of it all. I hope that my being there gave Gray Wolf some degree of comfort. Well, suffice it to say that I'm so glad that someone is helping Gray Wolf. I've been so worried about him. I drove to the jail—what do they call it? The correctional center?—anyway, I drove to the facility to see Gray Wolf, because you know the police always suspect the husband, and since Gray Wolf left home the next day, and hasn't been back, I thought he had been arrested. I took some magazines and other things—I think you would be as bored in jail as in the hospital, don't you?—but they, the jailers I mean, told me that there was no Gray Wolf Murphy there. They looked at me like I was a criminal! The jailers have such an attitude. Whatever happened to that old adage of innocent until proved guilty? Gray Wolf is innocent until the district attorney proves him guilty, and that hasn't happened yet. In fact, he hasn't even been arrested. It was a very unpleasant experience."

Peggy Otlander stopped to draw breath, took a sip of iced tea, sat the glass on an end table, and smiled at Megan. You couldn't fool her; she knew who was in charge of this investigative team. "I believe you wanted to ask me some questions. What do you want to know?" Peggy Otlander folded her hands and smiled at Megan again. Donna Reed with company.

Megan smiled back. She had a pained look on her face, probably from an earache. "Please tell us your impressions of Jessica Murphy."

Mrs. Otlander tucked a lock of hair behind her ear. "She was an attractive woman—blonde hair, green eyes, trim figure—with a sweet personality, but she wasn't a very happy woman. She was from somewhere back east, Illinois or Indiana maybe, some place where it rained more than here, and she was unhappy in the Panhandle. She loved the canyon—Palo Duro *is* beautiful—but she hated the dry prairie and the constant wind. I'm sure the wind blows in Illinois and Indiana, too, but she thought ours was stronger. Not everyone can tolerate the wind, you know. It makes some people very nervous. And she wasn't very happy with Gray Wolf, either, laughing at his calling himself a shaman. I was a little put out whenever she made fun of him. He is Comanche, some at least, a little bit maybe, and he enjoys learning about the Comanche culture. It's not against the law for a man to read about his heritage, is it? Of course, it isn't. But she hated it, and complained that he was gone so much. It still upsets me just thinking about her complaints. I don't know how she had time to notice that he wasn't there. She volunteered at the museum in Canyon and was friendly with Dr. Norman Ryland."

Megan choked on her tea.

After Peggy Otlander and I pounded Megan's back until she finally caught her breath, Mrs. Otlander got back to her impressions. "As I said, she was real friendly with Dr. Ryland. They had coffee in his office every time she worked at the museum, and she worked at least three times a week. Well, I'm a volunteer, too, and I didn't think it was a good idea for them to close his office door. It didn't look good, and sure enough, the whole museum staff gossiped about those two. But I don't know that there was as much talk about Jessica and Dr. Ryland as there was about her and Sam Reece. Jessica and Sam both loved hiking. Sam lives in that little Pueblo-style house about a hundred feet from the Murphys, so he could run down and knock on her door every time Gray Wolf was off being a shaman or lecturing about being a shaman. Then the two of them, Jessica and Sam I mean, would take a picnic basket and off they would go hiking. They would stay out all day when they went, and oh, but it made Sam's wife, Anita, furious. I was doing my walk—I take a short one every day, it's good for me—and I passed by the Reeces. Oh, my, but the yelling going on in that house. Really, these houses on the rim are all so close to one another, and the air is so clear, that it's easy to hear the neighbors, particularly if they're yelling at one another. It was a vicious argument, Dr. Clark, with Anita calling Sam some really horrible, filthy names. Anita's always been a plainspoken woman. And Jessica came in for her share of dirty names, too."

Ms. Otlander sipped her tea again, blotted her mouth with a napkin, and she was off and running—or talking I should say. "To my mind the most inexcusable behavior by Jessica was her going square dancing with William 'Good Deal Bill' Owens every weekend that Gray Wolf was out of town, and he was out of town a lot. Sometimes she wouldn't get back until the next day. She tried to tell me that they went out of town to Pampa or Dalhart or somewhere those weekends she didn't come home. She said it was easier to spend the night in whatever town than to drive back to Amarillo late at night. If Good Deal Will had been the only man she was friendly with, I would've probably believed her story. You know, even the best woman is going to fall if she is tempted every day and every day, don't you think, Dr. Clark?"

"She certainly had a lot of male friends," said Megan.

"I don't know why she didn't go with Gray Wolf on his trips. He told me about some of them, and they sounded like fun. He is such a sweet man, I don't know how she could treat him like that. It was terrible, terrible." She looked down at the floor for a moment, then lifted her head. Her eyes glistened with tears. "Maybe she wasn't so terrible, Dr. Clark. Maybe I'm remembering her wrong because Gray Wolf and I have become so close the last few years, and there was nothing we could do about it. It would so tawdry to live together when we didn't know where Jessica was, and we couldn't marry because we didn't know if she was dead or alive. If no trace of her turned up after seven years, Gray Wolf was planning to have her declared legally dead. After her turning up buried like that I feel guilty and I know he does, too. And I feel terrible for saying all the things about Jessica that I did, but I don't think lying would help Gray Wolf, do you, Dr. Clark?"

Megan reached over and squeezed Peggy Otlander's hand. "Lying won't help him at all, Peggy."

Peggy's eyes were wet. "Thank you, Dr. Clark, for not thinking badly of me." She blotted her eyes with her napkin and crushed it into a ball. "I'm talked out, and I can't think of anything else to say. If you could see yourselves out, I would appreciate it."

Megan and I walked to the door. "Thank you, Peggy," said Megan. "You were so much help." I wondered why Mrs. Otlander suddenly became Peggy.

Peggy Otlander nodded without turning. "I try to keep my eye on things. Sometimes I wish I didn't." I couldn't figure out how the woman had time to do anything else but spy on the neighbors.

Megan acted like she had discovered gold on the way back to Amarillo. "Nothing beats a gossip for help in a murder investigation. What a find Peggy Otlander is! And how sorry I felt for her."

I wasn't spending any sympathy on Peggy Otlander's romance with her shaman. I had other worries. "My opinion, for what it's worth, Megan, is there's no such thing as a platonic relationship between a man and a woman. Jessica Murphy was an affair waiting to happen, and one of her gentleman friends killed her, and he won't hesitate to kill you if you get too close to the truth."

"What do you mean there's no such thing as a platonic relationship between a man and a woman?" asked Megan.

"Just what I said. There is an inherent chemical reaction that occurs whenever a male and female spend too much time together. Call it a pheromonal attraction or hormones—"

"Pheromone is a form of hormone," interrupted Megan.

"Whatever. But you get my point, Megan. There's chemistry involved and it triggers a sexual reaction between male and female, so Jessica Murphy was playing with fire and if she hadn't been burned already, it was only a matter of time. In fact, I think she was already in bed with somebody and it wasn't the shaman. Otherwise, why murder her? So let's go dump our theories and Peggy Otlander's gossip in Jerry Carr's lap, and we're home free. Jerry will know everything we know, so there will be no reason for the killer to line you up in his sights because you'll no longer be hunting him."

I folded my arms and felt proud of myself. My denial of the existence of platonic relationships was based on logic, and constituted a backdoor approach to extracting Megan from her predicament. That is to say, to extract her from the middle of a murder investigation.

I waited for Megan's response. And waited. And waited.

I finally decided that my backdoor approach had been too subtle. "Don't you see, Megan, the murderer can only be one of two people: Sam Reece's wife, Anita, or Gray Wolf Murphy. Ergo, let Jerry Carr figure out which now that you can point him in the right direction. Don't you agree?"

"What about us?"

Finally, a response. "I'll take you to dinner after we talk to Jerry."

She looked at me, her face somber but the expression in her whiskey eyes was at least 180 proof. "If platonic relationships don't exist, then what kind of a relationship do we have? What will our chemistry lead to?"

I broke out in a sweat. "I wasn't talking about us."

"So we're the exception to the rule?"

I nodded my head as I surreptitiously dried my sweaty palms on my Levis. "Something like that."

"I see."

I wasn't about to ask her to clarify that two-word statement, so we left it at that.

We didn't stop by Special Crimes to talk to Jerry Carr, and I didn't insist. Sometimes it's better to leave well enough alone.

12

One of the things which danger does to you after a time is—well, to kill emotion. I don't think I shall ever feel anything again except fear. None of us can hate anymore—or love.

—D. in Graham Greene's
The Confidential Agent, 1939

PALO DURO CANYON, 1868

Spotted Tongue picked a chunk of buffalo meat out of the metal cooking pot. Green Willow always cut up the roasted buffalo meat and dropped it in the pot. He had heard Little Flower call it by the white man's name when he gave it to her after trading a horse to the Comancheros in exchange for it. What was the name? Fri pan? Something like that. He would never see the cooking pot again without seeing Little Flower's smile. She had even smiled at him, a slight smile that disappeared almost immediately. He ate more buffalo and hoped he could keep it down. His belly was still sick from grief. He thought about what he would do while he ate. Green Willow denied killing Little Flower. Wild Horse and Shaking Hand also denied killing her. He wiped his mouth on his arm and threw a half-chewed piece of meat on the ground. A yellow dog grabbed the meat and ran off, chased by several others. Little Flower didn't like his throwing bones and rotten meat near the arbor. He didn't understand her objections. When the camp began to stink too badly, then it was time to move. In the meantime the People just watched where they stepped.

He watched Green Willow sitting in her arbor still using her bone awl on the piece of buckskin. He wished he had something to do, a task that did not require thinking. He drew in a deep breath and wrinkled his nose. The camp did stink.

He saw Fat Belly walking toward him and lifted his hand in greeting. "Fat Belly, do Shaking Hand and Wild Horse still feel cold toward me?"

Fat Belly squatted down next to Spotted Tongue and leaned over to pick out a piece of buffalo meat. "My friend, your crazy charges came near to breaking the lifelong feeling that binds us together like sinew binds the flint to the shaft of the arrow. If anyone else had insulted Shaking Hand and Wild Horse like you did, they would have challenged you to fight them one at a time until one or the other was close to death. It'll be until the snows fly before the feelings will heal. I was sent to tell you these things."

"I said I was sorry and will pay compensation to Shaking Hand. What more can I do?"

"Leave them alone for at least a moon. Let them miss you."

"And if they do not miss me?"

"Life is hard, and walking backward in your moccasins won't change this morning." He pushed himself up, rubbed his belly, and called over to Green Willow. "That's good buffalo, Green Willow. If I'd had a bigger pony herd when you still lived in your parents's tipi, I would've outbid this foolish man. It's hard for me to be happy knowing I let such a good cook get away."

Green Willow laughed. "Fat Belly, if Slow Like a Turtle hears you say that, she'll burn up your food until you shrink like wet deer hide and your skin hangs loose and flaps in the wind."

Fat Belly shuddered and slapped his friend on the back. "Come, Spotted Tongue, let's talk to my first wife. Maybe she'll tell you that Coyote Dung murdered Little Flower. Him you can challenge for a fight to the death and few would care."

Spotted Tongue walked beside Fat Belly, hoping that he had not broken his friendships beyond his ability to fix them. "Fat Belly, did you ever see Coyote Dung near Little Flower?"

"I never saw her move away from your side when Coyote Dung was close. If Coyote Dung had struck her in the back of the head, he would have to fly above the ground because he cannot walk without making as much noise as a herd of buffalo. She would've heard him and cried out for you. And she would've fought him. Did she have any injuries except the killing wound, any that showed she had fought for her life?"

Spotted Tongue shook his head. "Her body was perfect except for the wound that broke her head."

"You make strong medicine, Spotted Tongue. Your medicine will show you the way to the evil one. Ah! Woman!" Fat Belly shouted at Slow Like a Turtle, ducking into the brush arbor and waving Spotted Tongue after him. "I brought a guest and friend."

Slow Like a Turtle, a tiny, slim girl who was formerly a Mexican captive, Fat Belly's wife was one of the few women who was friendly to Little Flower. They both had been taken away from their homes and families; they both were taken by their captors as wives. She caught Spotted Tongue's hands in her own. "Spotted Tongue, I grieve for you. She was so beautiful, like a brightly colored hummingbird. The People have lost a star in the night sky, but few know it."

Spotted Tongue squeezed Slow Like a Turtle's hands in friendship. "I thank you for me, but most of all I thank you in her name." He held his silence for a moment, thinking how to ask his questions so Slow Like a Turtle would not hold back through ignorance anything she knew. "My best friend's first wife who is also close to my heart, you were alone with Buffalo Woman and Little Flower after Green Willow returned to our arbor. Who else was there besides the three of you?"

Slow Like a Turtle thought a moment. "Wild Horse's wife, Deer Faun, and Shaking Hand's wife, Topay, were there, but they left before us. Buffalo Woman walked with me, and Little Flower stayed behind. She hadn't picked enough wild plums to fill her blanket, and she was afraid that Green Willow would be angry, so she stayed. I didn't worry about her running away because I knew her secret."

"What secret?" asked Spotted Tongue.

Slow Like a Turtle punched his arm. "The baby, you witless man! She told me about it."

"How? She didn't speak our tongue."

"She spoke my tongue, the one I spoke in Mexico when I was called Maria. She didn't speak it very well, but enough so I could understand her. And she used sign language. She wouldn't risk losing the baby by running away. Besides, you were the father. She wouldn't leave you. And yes, she told me all that, too," said Slow Like a Turtle, looking at him with sorrow.

"She would stay with me because she carried my son? She was accepting the ways of the Nermernuh?" asked Spotted Tongue, holding his breath.

"She said that you were a family, and she would become a Nerm because she couldn't be a Tejano any more. She didn't speak my tongue well enough to tell me why," said Slow Like a Turtle. "I would tell you that she wanted no

one but you, but I don't know. You killed her husband and I
think she had to forgive you before her heart could accept
any feelings for you. Coyote Dung killed her baby, that's
why he has always thought he had a claim to Little Flower,
and you stole her away. Him she hated. She often said
when you first brought her to us that she wished you and
Coyote Dung had left her alone. I told her that no man ever
asks a woman before he changes her life."

Spotted Tongue considered what Slow Like a Turtle told
him. He could see now that he didn't know Little Flower's
mind. She didn't accept the ways of the Nermernuh, and
maybe she never would have. But she would have lived with
him, and living in the same tipi and quickening with his sons
made fertile ground for a woman to grow close to a man.

He would think more about Little Flower later, after he
found and killed her murderer. Such justice would bring
peace to his mind. "Slow Like a Turtle, did you see anyone
else near the small canyon?"

She pursed her lips, then shook her head. "I saw no one
return to the little canyon, but I was thinking of all the work
waiting for me, drying the plums and slicing the buffalo before the meat begins to smell and looks green in the sun. I
was thinking of these things and others, and I wasn't paying
attention. I do know that no one passed us as we walked
along the path toward our arbors. If someone entered the little canyon after we left the path, I wouldn't notice. I looked
ahead toward my arbor, I never looked behind."

"Did you ever see Shaking Hand and Little Flower together?"

She smiled. "Yes! Shaking Hand would point to an object and say its name in our tongue. Little Flower would repeat the name backward and laugh. Or if Shaking Hand
pointed to an animal and said its name, Little Flower
would make the sound of the animal's voice. Shaking Hand

would stamp his feet and pull at his braids while Little Flower laughed. Then she might repeat the word perfectly and bow to everyone watching."

"Why did I never see that?" asked Spotted Tongue.

"I think she wanted to surprise you. That is the sense I made out of her speaking my tongue and using sign language."

"What of Wild Horse and Little Flower? Did they act honorably together?"

"Of course they did," answered Slow Like a Turtle, her face reflecting the confusion she felt. "Why do you ask about Wild Horse and Shaking Hand?"

Spotted Tongue answered her with some but not all of the truth. "I was jealous, and I wanted no one close to Little Flower but me."

"Spotted Tongue, he was only teaching her how to use a bow and arrow. He is the best of the People at fighting with the bow and arrow. She was proud of herself for learning and being so good, and Wild Horse was proud of her. He made her a fine bow and five arrows. He planned to let her surprise you with her skill. He wouldn't dishonor you."

He shook his fist at the sky. "Then who is lying? Someone is lying to me."

13

The best clues to a crime were in the characters of the people connected with it, and were worth all the burnt matches, footprints, or even fingerprints in the world.

—Solange Fontaine's favorite axiom,
"The Canary," in F. Tennyson Jesse's
The Solange Stories, 1931

PANHANDLE-PLAINS MUSEUM, PRESENT DAY

The guard at the museum's back door didn't exactly accuse Megan of lying, but he didn't exactly believe that she was meeting with Dr. Stevens and Dr. Ryland, either.

"I don't have a note about Dr. Ryland or Dr. Stevens having an appointment until this afternoon." The guard looked suspiciously at Megan. "You're not planning to visit the exhibits until this afternoon, are you?"

"My appointment is this morning."

"I can't let you in without paying if you're going to be walking around the museum until this afternoon, ma'am."

"I won't be viewing the exhibits all morning because my appointment is this morning," repeated Megan with what remained of a quickly diminishing store of patience.

"It's not right to be letting in some folks without paying

just because they claim they got an appointment this afternoon with Dr. Ryland."

Megan looked at the ceiling, then the floor while she took a firm grip on her temper. She had heard of "going by the book," but this guard sounded as if he was unable to express a single thought that didn't come directly from "the book." The museum must hire its guards according to how inflexible their personalities were. "Sir, would it be possible for you to call Dr. Ryland and tell him that Dr. Megan Clark is here for her ten o'clock appointment?"

The guard looked at a ruled sheet of paper on his desk with every line filled. "Dr. Ryland don't like to be bothered in the mornings unless I got to tell him that his appointment is here."

"He *does* have an appointment—with me, Dr. Megan Clark, Ph.D., so would you please call him?" This was too much when her mind was conflicted.

"He don't have any appointments until this afternoon. The schedule says so," said the guard, his chin jutting out and his eyes narrowed at this *person* who seemed determined to break his rules. Megan considered breaking the old man's neck except she always tried to treat the elderly with respect, not so much because such a tenet was a rule during her childhood, but because she admired the effort required to stay the course of a long life and arrive near the end with pride intact. Stubbornness, too, if this old man was any example.

The back door swung open, letting in a swirl of fallen leaves from the elm trees by the building, as well as Dr. Ryan Stevens, his hair sticking straight up on end from the wind, carrying a briefcase. "Megan! I'm sorry I'm late but I had to sign up students for appointments to discuss their subjects for term papers." He nodded to the guard as he set his briefcase on the desk and opened it. "Good morning, Henry. Feeling more like fall every day, isn't it?"

"Sure does, Professor," said Henry, relief on his face at seeing someone who knew the rules. "By the way, this young lady claims to have an appointment with you and Dr. Ryland, but there's nothing on the schedule until this afternoon. I'd let her in except she don't think she ought to pay admission when she says she's just here for an appointment, and according to the schedule she don't have any appointment this morning." He looked at Ryan with an expectant expression.

"I see," said Ryan, rubbing his hand across his mouth to hide a smile. "It's all right, Henry, I'll pay her admission. I'd hate to leave her sitting on the back steps until this afternoon, when she really does have an appointment this morning. I called Dr. Ryland at home last night to arrange a meeting with her and myself. He must have forgotten to tell you to add her name to the schedule."

"All right, Professor, as long as you vouch for her. I'm sorry I wouldn't let you in, ma'am, but people are always making up stories to try to get out of paying four dollars. You wouldn't believe some of them."

"I'm sure I wouldn't," said Megan, a grimace instead of a smile on her face. She handed Henry her four dollars. "I'll pay my own way. Dr. Stevens doesn't need to take care of me." She grabbed Ryan's coat sleeve. "Let's go! Thanks to Dr. Ryland's forgetfulness and Henry guarding the back door like Cerberus guarding the entrance to the underworld, I was barred from entering. And wouldn't you know it, I forgot my poppies and honey."

Ryan put his arm around her shoulders and walked her rapidly through the museum, around a corner and into the staff lounge. The door barely closed behind him before he fell into a shabby easy chair and started laughing. And laughing. "Didn't have an appointment," he kept repeating, followed by great whoops of laugher.

Megan debated what course of action she might take. This had been an out-of-control day from the moment she woke up and had to carry Rembrandt into the kitchen, until now. She had to take control of her life and this investigation. She couldn't interrogate a pompous ass when her assistant, her Watson, suffered from a case of the snickers. However, there was a cure for the snickers. She found a large glass and filled it with cold water, then hesitated. This was an extreme treatment, but she saw no indication that Ryan was anywhere near able to control himself, so she poured the water on his head.

Ryan uttered a word Megan considered inappropriate for use in a facility which encouraged tours by school children. She waited until Ryan had dried himself off with toilet paper, since the staff lounge was out of paper towels, before she spoke to him. "Are you feeling better?"

He glared at her while he peeled wet toilet paper off his cheek. "I wasn't feeling *bad* until you pulled that stunt."

"You were hysterical, so I administered a harmless form of shock therapy. Now that you're calm, let's get to our appointment before we're late." She studied his face. "You might want to pick the toilet paper out of your hair before we meet with Dr. Ryland. You don't want to embarrass yourself in front of a pompous ass, and if he's like other pompous asses I have known, he has no sense of humor."

She started for the door when he blocked it. He put his hands around her waist and lifted her up to sit on the counter. "What are you doing, Ryan? Put me down. Did that cold water chill your skull and interrupt your synapses?"

He rested his arms on her shoulders. "You've had a terrible two days, haven't you? And then the guard wouldn't

believe you have an appointment and wouldn't let you in
the museum unless you paid. Then when I finally get here,
you looked mad enough to cry. But do I offer sympathy?
No, I tease you and laugh at you. You are mad enough to
cry, aren't you?"

"Yes! There was that terrible article in the paper, and then
Jerry Carr ordered me around like I was some kid playing
Nancy Drew. I'm not Nancy Drew! Then Henry the Guard
treated me like I was a bimbo too stupid to tell time. He kept
saying that my appointment was this afternoon and insinuat-
ing I was cheating the museum out of four dollars! To top it
off, my best friend laughs at me."

Ryan handed her a handkerchief. "Am I really your best
friend?"

Megan blew her nose and blotted her eyes. "You know
you are."

He kissed her forehead. "I'm honored—and you are my
best friend. Now, will you tell me what is really wrong, because something is. Ordinarily, you would have called all
the TV and radio stations to refute that newspaper article.
You would have threatened to tell Jerry's mother that her
son was unkind to you, and then you would have eaten
Henry the Guard for breakfast. The only person you've put
in his place is me for laughing at you. When Megan Clark
doesn't give as good as she gets, I know something is
wrong. Will you tell me, honey?"

Megan swallowed and pressed her lips together until
she felt somewhat in control. "You know me too well."

"Well enough to know you're being evasive. Come on,
Megan, 'fess up."

"Rembrandt could barely walk this morning and he refused to eat and he can't drink. I have an appointment for
him with the vet this afternoon. I'm going to let him go. So
you see, I have more important *issues* to worry about than

four dollars' admission to the museum when I don't have time today to look at the exhibits, and you know how I feel about getting my money's worth."

Ryan lifted her off the counter and held her in his arms. "I'm sorry, honey. I'll drive you to the vet's so you can hold Rembrandt."

She cuddled up in his arms for an infusion of comfort, then gently pushed him away. Too much physical contact with Ryan made her uneasy. She liked it too much and was afraid that he would guess. After his lecture yesterday on pheromones and hormones and sexual chemistry and nonexistence of platonic relationships, she didn't want him sensing any ambiguity about her feelings toward him. Not that she could decipher her own feelings except that she didn't have a crush on him. Crushes were way too juvenile. Her uneasiness must be because Rembrandt would die this afternoon, and she needed to cling to Ryan for comfort. That made much more sense than the old cliché of suddenly falling in love with your best friend. That was so trite as to be embarrassing. And she was teary eyed again! Damnation!

She blotted her eyes and blew her nose for the second time. "If you don't mind, I'll keep your handkerchief, since we're"—she stopped and swallowed—"going to the vet's." She couldn't stand to say why again. She smiled at Ryan. At least she thought it was a smile. Her lips stretched at any rate. "Let's go beard the alley cat in his den."

He smiled at her. "Okay, but Megan, please remember that even pompous asses are dangerous at times."

"I'm up to it," she told him, straightening her shoulders, lifting her chin, and swearing a silent oath that she would tear Dr. Pompous Ass into tiny strips and turn him into jerky if he condescended to her.

Dr. Norman Ryland was built like a fireplug, round and

solid, and possessed of a strong sense of his own impor-
tance. He was a walking cliché: a black suit, white shirt, and
red power tie. Megan couldn't see his feet, but she would bet
he was wearing a pair of wingtips. His dress was too formal
for the Panhandle and particularly for working at the museum on a college campus where professors habitually wore
slacks and a casual shirt. She also noticed that Ryland sported
a haircut designed to minimize a receding hair line, with
"Mamie Eisenhower" bangs combed slightly to the side,
then sprayed to withstand gale-force winds. He was out
of place, and Megan suspected he had always been out of
place, the kid wearing the striped, long-sleeved shirt and
corduroy pants when all the other little boys wore T-shirts
and Levis.

"Ryan, I didn't know that you were acquainted with Dr.
Clark." Even Ryland's voice was out of place. Megan expected such a round, solidly build man to speak in a bari-
tone voice. He didn't. His voice was pure alto.

Ryan smiled and nodded, looking a little uneasy, like a
man wading in a river reputed to have quicksand. "She's
my neighbor."

The professor's smile at Ryan was best described as
prissy. "I'm sure Dr. Clark appreciates your company,
Ryan. Now that I think about it, I did hear that the two of
you spend your leisure time together."

Megan noticed that Ryland went from not knowing she
and Ryan were acquainted, to repeating gossip about how
much time they spent together.

Dr. Ryland didn't ask them to be seated, nor had he
risen when they entered the room, but relaxed in a high-
backed chair behind his gray metal desk. His furniture was
educational-issue which, at least, was more comfortable
than what Jerry Carr and his visitors endured. Without
waiting for an invitation, Megan sat down in a padded

metal chair. Ryan sat on a similar chair next to her, his face as blank as a statue on Easter Island. She shouldn't have asked him to come with her since he had to work with Ryland, but it was too late now. He was committed.

Megan waited for the good doctor to speak. Jerry Carr called silence a cop's best nonviolent tactic. Dr. Ryland justified Jerry's faith in tactics by rushing in to fill the silence.

"What is your purpose in talking to me?" he asked, thick fingers tapping on his desk.

"I believe that Jessica Murphy was a volunteer at the museum?" asked Megan. She hated people who tapped their fingers while she was talking to them. It was just plain rude.

"Yes, she was. She was a most gracious and cultured woman who shared my deep interest in oriental porcelain. She had superb taste, superb. Such a wonderful woman and so knowledgeable about Chinese porcelain. We talked for hours. Her death is such a loss to scholarship." He wiped his eyes although Megan didn't notice that he had shed any tears. "I think of her often and miss her still. Wonderful woman. Wonderful."

"I'm sure she was a fine woman," said Megan, taking a small notebook and pen out of her purse. "We understand that you spent a lot of time alone with Mrs. Murphy?"

Dr. Ryland stopped his show of grief, and stared at her with suspicion. "Are you accusing me of improper behavior?"

"No. I'm saying that according to my source, you and Ms. Murphy spent a lot of time alone—in this office—with the door closed," said Megan, drawing out her statement until Ryland flinched. "I was double-checking the veracity of my source."

"I demand to know your source because that person is slandering me." He slammed his fist on his desktop. Megan hated that kind of behavior, too. It was the adult version of lying on the floor and kicking your feet.

"I don't think so, since you've already admitted that you 'talked for hours.' What I want to know is the extent of your intimacy with Jessica." Megan jotted a few notes in her notebook.

Dr. Ryland looked at Ryan to see if he had any reaction to her question. Ryan's face was still blank, although he might be a bit paler than when they came in. Seeing no help from that quarter, Dr. Ryland drew himself up as much as a man shaped like a fireplug could. "Mrs. Murphy and I were not intimate. Anyone who says we were is lying."

"That's certainly possible, Dr. Ryland," said Ryan. "Don't you agree, Megan?"

Megan didn't agree but she let Ryan's feeble attempt at conciliation pass without saying so. "Did you attempt intimacy and Mrs. Murphy rebuffed you? Did you harass her?"

"No! I did not attempt intimacy! I did not harass her." Dr. Ryland wiped his sweaty forehead. "And what are you writing? Are you making notes of this conversation? I demand you stop!"

Ryan smiled at Dr. Ryland. "After all, we don't know these people. We don't have any failsafe way of gauging their truthfulness. Do we, Megan?"

"Did Jessica threaten to tell her husband?"

"Do we, Megan?" shouted Ryan.

"No! She didn't threaten to tell her husband! There was nothing to tell her husband." Ryland was turning a light shade of red. "And I demand to see what you are writing!" Again ignoring his demand, Megan decided to see if his face would turn a darker red.

"Megan! There's no call to make accusations against Dr. Ryland without proof."

Megan wished Ryan would butt out. "So you went to see Jessica. Did you bring the knife with you, or did you use one you found in her home?" She jotted a few words in her notebook again.

"Why are you accusing me of such horrible acts?" He sounded self-pitying rather than indignant. Megan wondered why. Self-pity is not synonymous with denial.

"Then did you tip Jessica's body over the rim into the canyon? Did you walk up Little Sunday Canyon with a shovel and bury Jessica under Indian Rock? You didn't think Indian Rock would ever move, did you? A room-sized rock? It must have been a terrible shock to see that it did, indeed, move. 'How easily murder is discovered!' Tamora, *Titus Andronicus,* Act II, scene iii. It's written by Shakespeare. I'm sure you've heard of him."

"No! No! No! And no again!"

Megan opened her eyes as widely as she could and raised her eyebrows in a parody of surprise. "You haven't heard of Shakespeare? I'm surprised. He's quite well known."

"No! No! No!"

Megan expected to see him stamp his foot. "You've neglected your education if you've never read Shakespeare. You should get by the library more often."

Dr. Ryland looked desperate. "Yes! Yes! Of course I know Shakespeare. I was saying no to all your accusations."

Megan dredged up the best expression of fake sympathy she was capable of. "I'm glad. Better a murderer than a sexual predator. More respectable, don't you agree?"

"Megan, can we step outside for a minute? I need to talk to you," said Ryan.

"In a minute, Ryan!" said Megan, glaring at him before turning back to smile at the professor.

Dr. Ryland was sweaty, and his face had darkened to a

lovely shade of puce. He rose and leaned over the desk. "Why are you doing this to me?"

"Did you check on Indian Rock every day or every week or every month?" asked Megan, her pen poised over her notebook.

"No! No! Please leave me alone." Ryland stumbled around the desk and seized Ryan's arm. "Dr. Stevens! Are you going to let her talk to a fellow professor like that?"

Ryan looked thoughtful and studied the ceiling in search of an answer while he peeled Ryland's grasping fingers off his arm. "Free speech is protected by the Bill of Rights to the Constitution. Besides, Megan doesn't take to being told what to do—or say. She's a woman of independent spirit with a large measure of stubbornness. No, Dr. Ryland, I don't *let* Dr. Clark talk. I just stay quiet when she does. I recommend you do the same. Eventually, she tires of asking questions no one will answer."

Megan stood up. Time to leave before the good professor had a stroke. She had a few remarks to make to Ryan, too. "We'll leave you alone for now, Dr. Ryland, but we'll be back."

Ryland trailed after her. "Please, don't come back. Why are you coming back?"

"Because you lied to me," said Megan, glancing down at his shoes. She was right. Wingtips.

14

The terrier does not give the rat time to dig a hole.

—Jacques-the-Odd to Detective-Sergeant
George Ormerod in Leslie Thomas's
Ormerod's Landing, 1978

PANHANDLE-PLAINS MUSEUM, PRESENT DAY

"What was Ryland lying about, Megan?" I asked as we walked by Henry the Guard's booth and out the museum's back door. The coming trip to the vet must be weighing on her mind, because she took a long time answering as we stood by her black behemoth.

"I'm not sure that he is. I accused him to see how much more he would tell us in an attempt to persuade us that he's telling the truth. Have you ever noticed that about people, Ryan? That a liar will talk and talk and often contradicts himself in an effort to fool the listener? And our good professor did contradict himself. He denied that he and Jessica Murphy were together all that much, when, in fact, he said they talked for hours. Did you notice he became flustered when I pointed out his inconsistency?"

"He was certainly flustered by all your remarks about Shakespeare," I said with disapproval.

"He was, wasn't he? That's why I did it. I want him

flustered and uncertain about what questions I might ask next time."

"You had the whole scenario planned, didn't you, Megan. And what do you mean, next time? I don't think I can sit through another one of your interrogations, particularly of Dr. Ryland. I actually felt sorry for him by the time we left."

"I didn't plan the Shakespeare bit, Ryan. You can't *plan* an exchange like that! I sort of improvised when I saw an opportunity. And you don't approve, do you?"

"No, I don't."

I had disapproved of Megan's behavior in the past—breaking and entering, for example, and setting a trap for a murderer—but this time was different. She humiliated Dr. Ryland, and I didn't believe her means justified this particular end. I supported her while we were in Ryland's office—at least, I didn't gag her with her own notebook—but I'd be damned if I would support any such tactics again. It occurred to me that I wouldn't want to get into a verbal battle with Megan Clark. She would have no mercy.

Megan's face revealed a variety of expressions: shock, disappointment, hurt, and finally, anger. "If you disapprove of my behavior, then you can stay at home while I go question Sam Reece. I can function without your constant presence. And your constant interruptions." She climbed into the behemoth and slammed the door.

I jerked open the truck door and grabbed the steering wheel. "Sam and Anita Reece are friends of mine, too!"

Megan tried to force my hand away from the steering wheel. "I've never heard you mention the Reeces. Besides, Sam Reece is a lawyer, and you don't like lawyers."

I hung onto the steering wheel. "All right! The Reeces are acquaintances, but I do know them. If you keep up this kind of behavior I won't be able to show my face in the museum or in Amarillo. Besides, questioning a lawyer is like waving a red flag at a bull. Reece will retaliate."

Megan let go of my hand and twisted around on the seat. "But Ryan, Gray Wolf Murphy asked me for help, and I agreed to help find Jessica's murderer so our shaman won't be arrested. I need your help." She cupped my face with her hands, and I felt my determination leaking away. "Please, Ryan, my best friend, help me."

I looked into those whiskey-colored eyes and swallowed. She was creating another predicament. "I'll go with you."

I drove to Sam Reece's law offices. I didn't judge Megan able to drive after taking Rembrandt to the vet's. She insisted on holding the beagle while the vet administered the injection because she didn't want Rembrandt to believe she was abandoning him to die. She hadn't cried yet and that frightened me. At some point she would shatter like a fragile piece of crystal in an earthquake. I only hope I'm around to hold her. Not that I want to deny her mother the opportunity to succor her daughter, but Megan's mother is like Mount Rushmore: awe-inspiring but not what you'd choose for artwork in a cozy bedroom. She tries hard at motherhood, but she is to Donna Reed what PETA is to a T-bone steak. She's into causes; she can orchestrate a demonstration like nobody's business in support of clean air, clean water, save the earth, save the rain forest, save the whales. All those causes are worthy of my support to a greater or lesser degree, but Megan's mother works in generalities: all or nothing, one-size-fits-all. A child is a very specific creature. Thank God Megan and her mother lived next to us, so my wife could provide the milk-and-cookies ingredient to Megan's childhood. Megan's rearing goes a long way toward explaining her character: the high ideals that fuel her uncompromising belief in justice, her willingness to risk her life to save the innocent, and her unselfish love for the small and helpless that makes her hold a little animal in her arms while it dies. I favor the unselfish love part of her over her belief in abstracts; the world is lacking enough unselfish love.

It was obvious to me from the expression on Sam Reece's face that if he believed in high ideals and unselfish love, fear sidetracked both character traits. He wasn't a pompous ass; just a lawyer in conflict between his feelings for Jessica and his desire to save his own skin.

"I don't know how I can help you in your investigation, Dr. Clark, Dr. Stevens," said Reece. "We are neighbors of the Murphys, but not on intimate terms with them. Gray Wolf was out of town frequently in his capacity as a medicine man for the Comanches—"

"Shaman," I said. "Shaman is the preferred term for what Murphy is attempting. A medicine man is primarily a healer while a shaman is a medium between the visible and the invisible spirit world. The Comanche actually didn't have shamans as we define the term until very late in their existence as a free culture. And it's a free country, so Gray Wolf Murphy can be a shaman if he chooses."

Reece's smile came and went like the Cheshire cat's. "I see. Well, I don't deal with the spirit world, so I'm unaware of the proper terminology. To continue, Gray Wolf was frequently out of town in his capacity as a *shaman*"—a Cheshire cat's smile appeared again—"for the Comanches, so we weren't able to associate with them as couples."

"You associated with Jessica, Mr. Reece, so from my perspective the two of you were a 'couple.' Isn't that true?" asked Megan, removing her notebook and pen from her purse. Her voice sounded flat, so I knew she was still emotionally numb from giving up Rembrandt.

"We both enjoyed hiking in the canyon. She would often walk down to my home and knock on the door to invite me to go hiking with her. She felt a woman alone was vulnerable out in the wild. Most of the time I'd change into my hiking gear and away we'd go." The Cheshire cat disappeared. After observing Reece even a short while, I noticed he was taking more care with his answers. Not lying exactly, but omitting part of the truth. In political parlance, no smile equaled a spin on his statements.

Megan sat back in a maroon leather wing chair identical to the maroon leather chair I sat on. "Would you care to revise your first statement on hiking?" She jotted down a note.

That pesky Cheshire cat was back. "You mean about enjoying hiking?" asked Reece, clearly puzzled at the direction her questions were taking, but stretching his neck to peer at her notebook nonetheless.

"No, I meant your first response to my question about you and Jessica being a couple."

"Oh, I understand. You're considering my response in its totality." Clever evasion, but he was a lawyer after all.

"Yes," she said and waited, a tactic she used with great success this morning on Dr. Ryland.

Used to using the silence tactic himself in the courtroom, Reece also waited, but he was the one on the hot seat, so he capitulated first. "I wouldn't consider Jessica and I as a couple."

"What would you consider her, Mr. Reece?" asked Megan, making another note.

"A friend, a good friend." The Cheshire cat was back, so he must be telling the absolute truth.

"Do you often spend all day hiking alone with a woman friend?"

"Now that I think about it, no, I don't." Still smiling.

"So the two of you together, alone, all day, wouldn't you consider yourselves a couple?"

Reece shifted on his high-backed chair. The Cheshire cat was gone, and he was really nervous. "I guess, in a strict mathematical sense, since there were two of us, and by definition couple means two."

"What was your wife's opinion of these hiking trips when you were part of a couple, but she wasn't the other half?" asked Megan, her pen poised over her notebook.

The cat was nowhere in sight, and Reece wouldn't meet Megan's eyes. That didn't denote shame, but another attempt to squint at her notebook. "She, she was fine with it. She knew how much I enjoyed hiking."

"I understand that you and your wife had a violent argument on the subject of Jessica Murphy and your 'hikes,' especially the all-day, picnic ones. Is that true?"

"My wife and I did have a disagreement, but she wanted to go to a movie, a chick flick, and I didn't want to go and I told her so." Very solemn face.

"After five years you still remember that you were fighting over a chick flick?"

"I have an excellent memory, Dr. Clark." His smirk reminded me of Randel's.

"How many years have you and your wife been married, Mr. Reece?"

"Fifteen wonderful years." That smirk again. I prefer the Cheshire cat.

"I congratulate you," said Megan, inclining her chin in a royal gesture.

"Thank you, Dr. Clark," replied Reece, inclining his chin in a conscious image of hers.

"Fifteen years of matrimony and you and your wife have only argued once, and over a chick flick at that."

Reece leaned back in his chair, a expression of respect

quickly replaced by one of chagrin. "You would have made a formidable attorney, Dr. Clark."

"Would you care to search your memory again, Mr. Reece? My sources reported a 'violent' argument," said Megan, crossing her legs and resting her notebook on one knee.

"Who are your sources?" demanded Reece with a wide grin. The cat was back.

"I am a legal assistant to Herb Jackson III. My interviews are confidential. Care to answer the question? Did you have a violent argument with your wife on the subject of Jessica Murphy?" Megan waited, her pen poised over her notebook.

Reece smirked. "Not to the best of my recollection."

"Another question. Did you make love to Jessica Murphy while on your hiking trips?" She made a quick note, then looked back at him with a smirk of her own.

He didn't know whether to smile or not, so the Cheshire cat kept flashing on and off like a vacancy sign at a cheap motel. "No, I did not. Jessica was not that kind of woman."

"Then she rebuffed you?"

"No! I gave her no reason to rebuff me." The cat was back, and I wondered why.

"Did you bring your own knife or use one of Jessica's?" She made a quick note with the pen.

"No! I didn't take a knife to Jessica's." Wide grin. I wondered if I was misinterpreting the negative for the positive.

"So you used one of hers?"

"No, damn it! Where are you getting this stuff?"

"Were you surprised when Indian Rock rolled enough to reveal Jessica's grave?"

"I was surprised she was buried there. I mean, I didn't know her grave was there." Off and on, off and on with the smile.

"If you kept careful watch on Indian Rock, how did you

miss its moving to reveal Jessica's grave? I mean, my God, her skeleton was in plain view." Megan's voice was no longer flat.

"I have no more comments to make," said Reece, folding his arms. "You can find your own way out. If you loiter in the lobby, I will call security." He was definitely not lying.

We left. Megan had a grin on her face. "He's lying."

"I wouldn't put it past either Sam Reece or Norman Ryland to at least be having a minor affair with Jessica Murphy."

She laughed. "A minor affair, Ryan? What constitutes a minor affair? A kiss on the cheek? Or does it go as far at stroking a woman's breasts?"

I felt my face turn bright red. I tried to talk, but I was stuttering too much. My God, Megan and I have never been so specific about body parts. I was embarrassed—and wanted to stare at Megan's assets since she brought up the subject. I needed a cold shower and a tall drink.

10 pg

15

*Detection requires a patient persistence which amounts
to obstinacy.*

—Chief Superintendent Adam Dalgleish
in P. D. James's *An Unsuitable Job for a Woman*, 1972

PALO DURO CANYON, 1868

"Wild Horse."

Dressed only in his breechclout Wild Horse sat on a
trade blanket in his brush arbor next to Deer Fawn, who
was lying curled up on her side. Her eyes were closed and
one hand rested on the side of her big belly. At the sound of
his voice, she opened her eyes, saw him and struggled to
sit up, but Wild Horse pressed her back on the blanket. He
whispered something to her, then got to his feet and ducked
out of his arbor, forcing Spotted Tongue to stumble backward several steps before he found his feet again. Spotted
Tongue flinched when he saw the expression on his friend's
face.

"Didn't Fat Belly talk to you?" asked Wild Horse, pushing him backward with a hand on Spotted Tongue's chest.

Spotted Tongue stumbled back again, stepped on a pile
of slick, wild plum pits and fought for his balance to save
himself from looking the fool. "Fat Belly brought me your
words, but I can do nothing to give you back your honor

except to give you words of my own along with my horses. I lost my wits from my grief and hurt you. When I did, I hurt my own heart." He thought he saw Wild Horse's face lose its anger and felt hope that he tied the break in their friendship back together again. He felt his own face and body lose their stiffness and wiped the sweat from his brow. It was cold. He had not realized how afraid he was that he could not repair what he had broken.

"I would obey yours and Shaking Hand's words, Wild Horse. I would take my face out of your sight until you called me back if I could, but I can't. I have more questions for you, and I must talk to Deer Fawn."

Wild Horse's eyes grew round, then narrowed into slits until Spotted Tongue couldn't see what feelings lay in his friend's heart. But he didn't need to see what feelings Wild Horse's eyes revealed; he knew. He didn't see the other warrior's move, just felt himself falling backward and a numbing pain in his chest where Wild Horse's fist had hit him.

"You son of scabby Tejano woman with crooked eyes, are you too witless to understand the Nermernuh tongue? Are your ears full of the dung of a rat? Would you eat your friends's hearts like a filthy Tonkawa and leave us no feelings for you at all." With his last words Wild Horse kicked Spotted Tongue in the side.

Spotted Tongue grabbed his side as the hot pain of his already broken ribs joined with the new pain that throbbed just below his ribs. He held in his scream. A Nerm does not cry from pain. If a Nerm was allowed to scream, Spotted Tongue thought his would be heard all the way to the tall thick trees that grew many days' ride toward the east. Instead, he laid at Wild Horse's feet and listened to his curses, as did the large crowd of the Nermernuh gathered around them. Wild Horse's cursing was admired by all the Nermernuh. No one else could string together insults like

him. When he finally ran out of breath and curses, Wild
Horse leaned over and rested his hands on his knees. His
chin was at the right height for Spotted Tongue to reach
with his foot. He kicked Wild Horse over backward. The
warrior landed on his back with a thud that stole his breath
away. Spotted Tongue rolled over to his hands and knees
and struggled to stand up, accepting the pain as a band of
fire around his chest. Someone's hands grabbed him under
the arms and lifted him to his feet.

"Wild Horse is right. You're witless" said Fat Belly.
"How many more times will you lose a fight? First it was
Coyote Dung, now it is Wild Horse. How many bones will
you break by speaking when you should wait. You're like a
bear after honey; you don't care how many times you are
stung. I told you Wild Horse's words and Shaking Hand's,
too. Are your ears open?

"Not according to Wild Horse." Spotted Tongue's laugh
sounded shaky to his own ears.

"The fight is over and Wild Horse has used all his
curses," Fat Belly called to the Nermernuh gathered to watch
the two friends and wonder if their friendship was no more.
"Go back to your arbors or your wives or your gambling.
There's nothing more here to see." The big-bellied warrior
turned back to Spotted Tongue. "Why are you here at Wild
Horse's arbor? Will you throw away your friends when all
you need is patience to save their friendship? Loosen your
tongue, Spotted Tongue and talk to me."

Wild Horse answered for him. The stocky warrior pointed
to Spotted Tongue. "He has more questions for me. I told
him that I did not kill Little Flower, and he still would ask
questions of me. But that is not all. He wants to ask Deer
Fawn questions. Her belly is bigger than yours with my son,
and he wants to pester her. I will not let him talk to her."

Spotted Tongue felt a growing feeling of desperation.

Wild Horse didn't understand. But he must understand. "I must talk to her, Wild Horse. I must know what she saw in the canyon. I need to know who was the last person to walk out of the canyon. I would not bother her so close to her time, but I have to know what she knows. Murder has been done to a Nerm."

"She was a slave who hated the Nermernuh and made you pant like a dog at her feet." Deer Fawn's voice rose above the sounds of the three men.

"Little Flower was my second wife. That made her a Nerm." Spotted Tongue was weary of explaining. No one listened. Of course, Deer Fawn would always take an idea and never give it up even if she was proved wrong. If she were not married to a great warrior like Wild Horse, no one would want her company. As it was, no one wanted to show disrespect to Wild Horse.

"She hated us," said Deer Fawn, folding her arms and sticking out her bottom lip in a pout.

"Go back into the arbor and lay down. I forbid you to talk to Spotted Tongue. I'll not have you crying again," said Wild Horse. Even he looked like he was running out of patience.

"Why did you cry, Deer Fawn?" asked Spotted Tongue. He had learned to ask one small question at a time, then listen to the words with his ears, and listen to what they mean with his heart.

Wild Horse pulled his knife and stood before Spotted Tongue in a half-crouch. "I will not kill you, but I will bleed you, so you will know next time not to attack my honor and to approach against my wishes—"

Fat Belly gripped Wild Horse's wrist and twisted it until the warrior dropped his knife. "There'll be none of that. The Nermernuh do not fight each other. How will we heal our wounded friendships if we kill each other?"

"*Maybe* I *do not want to heal the friendship,*" said Wild Horse. "*Maybe* I *want to go before the council and ask for a fight to the death. If he's dead, I don't have to worry about his friendship.*"

"*Don't talk foolishness!*" said Fat Belly. "*The vote in council must be unanimous, and I will vote against you. If the vote goes against you and you fight and kill Spotted Tongue anyway, you will be cast out of our band. If Spotted Tongue kills you, then he is outcast. You will die on the prairie by yourself.*"

"*I will vote with Fat Belly,*" said Shaking Hand. He had been standing behind Fat Belly eating a plum and listening. He was patient, waiting to make up his mind until he thought about it. He spit out the pit and wiped his sticky hands on his breechclout. "*We will not kill each other. What is the matter with you, Wild Horse, Spotted Tongue? You act like the Comancheros on fire water. You act crazy. Wild Horse, will you fight Spotted Tongue when grief eats up his wits, so he doesn't know friend from enemy; when his wife is murdered, but he knows the Nermernuh do not murder each other. But a Nerm did murder Little Flower, and Spotted Tongue must find that killer.*"

"*I will not let him to speak to Deer Fawn. Once she delivers my son, then he may talk to her until his tongue falls out,*" said Wild Horse, his chin jutting out with stubbornness.

Spotted Tongue decided that Wild Horse and his wife were much alike in holding on to one idea. "*I need to talk to her now. In another moon or so anything can happen. Who is to say that Little Flower is the only Nerm who will die. A Nerm who lacks enough honor to kill another Nerm is not to be ignored. Such evil will only grow greater each year.*"

Fat Belly stood with his arms folded, thinking. "*Wild Horse, you will allow Spotted Tongue to ask you his*

*questions. Spotted Tongue, you may not question Deer
Fawn until she delivers."*

"You act like you're a chief," said Wild Horse. "You're
not. The only warriors to give orders to the Nermernuh are
a war chief, and the chief who keeps order in the council.
Otherwise, we are free to act as we want as long we don't
break taboos and remember the courtesies of the Nermernuh. That is the way of the People."

"I obey Fat Belly's orders," said Spotted Tongue. "He
isn't a chief, but all of us trust him to be fair and never to
lie. Is there anything else we could ask for in a chief to settle our differences?"

Wild Horse looked from Fat Belly and Shaking Hand to
Spotted Tongue and back again, then seemed to make up
his mind. His face looked pinched, as though he had eaten
a sour plum. He nodded his head. "All right, I will answer
his questions. At least he won't be bothering my wife while
she is carrying my son." He turned to Spotted Tongue.
"Ask your questions and I'll answer them."

Spotted Tongue hoped Wild Horse ended up having a
daughter. "Where were you at the time Deer Fawn left your
arbor to pick plums with the other women?"

Wild Horse frowned, drew a deep breath, and started
talking. "I saw Deer Fawn leave, and I got up to make water in back of our brush arbor. Then I laid down again.
Last night's celebration of the raid went on until very late.
I was tired. When I got up, I ate some buffalo from the cook
pot, then took my dice and asked Shaking Hand and Fat
Belly to join me for a game. I was there until you interrupted with your questions."

"Did anybody see you when you were sleeping in your
arbor?" asked Spotted Tongue.

Wild Horse threw up his hands. "If I was asleep, then I
wouldn't know who saw me.

Spotted Tongue felt the blood heat his face. He didn't know how to search for a murderer. He seemed to be the fool each time he asked a question. Maybe that was good; maybe those he questioned might let slip information because they thought him a fool. It was that or torture the information out of those he suspected, and he never was comfortable around torture. Just one more way he was different from the Nermernuh.

Spotted Tongue shrugged. "It was stupid to ask you. Fat Belly, did you or Shaking Hand see Wild Horse?"

"I didn't need to see him," said Shaking Hand. "I could hear him. He shook the ground like a herd of buffalo running."

Fat Belly laughed. "I believe you. I never sleep next to him on raids. I remember once even a captive complained. Are you satisfied, Spotted Tongue?"

Spotted Tongue nodded, then turned to Shaking Hand. "Where were you?

"If I could hear Wild Horse, then I had to be in camp. I was boiling coffee that I traded for with the Comencheros the last time we met with them. I had just enough coffee to make two cups. I gave one to Fat Belly."

"Why didn't you give it to me?" asked Wild Horse.

"Fat Belly always has sugar left from trading, and we both like a lot of sugar."

Fat Belly agreed. "I had a cup of coffee with Shaking Hand. I saw you run out of your arbor like a dog with its tail on fire. You know where I was after that. I heard you and Coyote Dung fighting and went to save you."

"I didn't remember it like that," said Spotted Tongue.

Fat Belly arched his eyebrows. "You've a bad memory."

"Shaking Hand, I need to talk to Topay," said Spotted Tongue.

Shaking Hand's mouth was stuffed with wild plums. He

spit out another pit. "Come on, then. Let's get it over with."
They walked past two arbors before Shaking Hand caught
Spotted Tongue's arm. "Wait. I want to warn you. Don't
believe everything Topay says. She is mad enough to scalp
me over my teaching our tongue to Little Flower. I didn't
think to tell her. I don't tell my wife everything I do."

At least the story Buffalo Woman told Spotted Tongue
was true. Would that everyone's words were true. "I was
feeling like a fool, but you are a bigger one. Didn't you
know she would find out?"

They walked to the next arbor. "At least she can't move
back into her parents' tipi because Mexico is many, many
days ride. She just will scream at me in her tongue, and I
only speak a few words. I think next raid I'll look out for
another woman. Then I'll tell Topay to build her own arbor.
If I want her, I'll pull on the string around her wrist, and
I'll only want her if she is in a laughing mood."

Spotted Tongue always thought that Topay was a pretty
woman. She had light skin where the sun didn't burn her,
and her hair wasn't black like most Mexicans, but a dark
brown that shined with red in the sunlight. She was taller
than Slow Like a Turtle, about as tall as Shaking Hand. No
woman in the band was as tall as Little Flower had been,
just like no man was as tall as himself.

Topay sat in front of the arbor she shared with Shaking
Hand. The ground around the arbor was clean as Topay
was impatient with the People's habit of throwing scraps
around the arbor or the tipi in winter. In that she was like
Little Flower. He didn't understand Topay just like he
hadn't understood Little Flower.

"Topay, I need to talk to you—"

"I know. What did I see in the canyon? I walked out with
Buffalo Woman because I didn't want to walk with Deer
Fawn. She complains too much. All the time complains.

Her tongue should have blisters. Wild Horse must stick buckskin in his ears to live with that woman. I sat down in the shade of a tree and waited until that woman was out of hearing distance, my hearing. And before you ask, no one passed Buffalo Woman and me going the other way up the canyon."

"Who else walked with you besides Buffalo Woman?"

"No one else. Buffalo Woman walked beside me. Deer Fawn was ahead of us—way ahead—talking to herself because no one else would walk with her. That is all I know, Spotted Tongue. Now I must talk to Shaking Hand. I have heard he wants a second wife to share his blankets, and for me to move into my own tipi. I do not like to hear such talk and I will tell Shaking Hand so."

If Spotted Tongue was not searching for a murderer, he would stay to watch Shaking Hand try to make peace with Topay. The two would cause much laughter among the Nermernuh. But he walked back to his own brush arbor instead. Someone was lying. But he didn't feel the lie from anyone. Maybe he should force them to look into his eyes and tell their stories again. No one could meet his eyes and lie since he lost his medicine. But if he did that, too many people would be afraid and start fearing him. Before too long they would cast him out because he frightened them too much, and they would believe he had an evil spirit in him. He didn't have an evil spirit and he wasn't going to risk the Nermernuh believing any such lies about him. He didn't know what had happened to himself, and he didn't know why it had happened. He didn't know if one day he would walk into the prairie and discover he could make medicine again. What frightened him most of all was the question that weighed on his mind the nights he couldn't sleep, or days when he would be riding his pony in the hot sun: Did he want his medicine back now that he knew it made no difference?

Buffalo Woman sat with Green Willow in front of his brush arbor cutting pits out of the wild plums and dropping the plums on a flat rock from the stream. They would later crush them along with grapes and nuts and whatever else to make pemmican for the winter. If the People ran out of dried buffalo meat and couldn't track down any fresh meat, then the Nermernuh could eat pemmican. He picked up a plum and ate it. Green Willow was right, the plums were as sweet as any Spotted Tongue could remember.

"Spotted Tongue, have you learned anything?" asked Buffalo Woman. "Green Willow and I were just talking about the murder of Little Flower and wondering if the murderer is still hiding from you."

"I have learned nothing except no one could have killed Little Flower. And that is impossible. She didn't murder herself."

"Maybe you should find out first why somebody murdered Little Flower, husband," said Green Willow. "If you learn why each person would want her dead, then maybe you can cast out some of the people and look harder at who is left."

Of all the women Spotted Tongue had talked to all day, Green Willow might be the smartest.

Not Ryan

16

Haven't you sometimes felt, when you've been sick or tired or worried, that sanity was like a tightrope strung across a great gulf, that you have to walk over it and if the slightest little adjustment should go wrong you'd topple off and never stop falling?

—Harold Forster in Samuel Rogers's
Don't Look Behind You!, 1944

LITTLE SUNDAY CANYON, PRESENT DAY

"I don't know why we didn't talk to Anita Reece when we were already here the other day talking to Peggy Otlander," grumbled Ryan.

"Because wives call their husbands about strangers coming to their doors and asking personal questions, but husbands don't often call their wives about the strangers coming to their offices asking personal questions. That's why," finished Megan, folding her arms and waiting for the next complaint from Ryan. For some reason he was in a bad mood and had been since they—all right, she—questioned the good professor.

She watched Ryan mulling over her comment, probably trying to decide if it was a sexist remark.

"Meaning if we had talked to Anita Reece first, she would have called Sam by the time her front door hit our behinds," Ryan finally said. "And Sam would either have been prepared for us, or he would have thrown us out. This way there's a chance that Anita Reece knows nothing about our amateur sleuthing that's going to get us killed one day."

"You're exaggerating again. We're perfectly safe from this murderer. Neither of us is alone in this endeavor. If I disappeared, you would know exactly where I was going and you would call Jerry Carr who, after cursing me for interfering in a police matter, would immediately pounce on whatever suspect I was with. The same would be true if you disappeared, so our suspects would know their chances of being caught are very, very high. I have deduced that our murderer is imaginative, but he or she took advantage of opportunities—Gray Wolf leaving Jessica alone for long periods—that simply won't be there in reference to us. So I have further deduced that we and the book club are safe from murder on this case. You can't think that I have failed to calculate the odds of our turning up in shallow graves in Palo Duro Canyon?"

She noticed that Ryan's face had lost its healthy flush during the course of her explanation and was now as pale as her white silk blouse. "I'm glad to hear how safe we'll be. I hope you've shared this information with our suspects, or are we depending on their being able to figure it out for themselves? Because I think you're underestimating the cunning of this murderer. Anyone with the *cajones* to kill Jessica Murphy, bury her in a shallow grave, and go on about his or her business for *five* years without anyone being suspicious is one smart *hombre* who wouldn't hesitate a moment to introduce you to a sharp knife." Ryan's voice gradually grew louder until he finished his warning in a shout.

Megan flinched. "Your pickup's cab is a little too small for you to be shouting. I have very sensitive ears."

"Be glad you're alive to hear," he said, turning onto the gravel road that ran through the pasture and ended at the small group of houses that lined the rim of Little Sunday Canyon.

"Sarcasm is the last weapon of one who has lost an argument. And don't say anything else, just listen to me. After I received Gray Wolf's list of friends, family, and neighbors, we lucked out by finding out gossip first thing. Talking to Peggy, we learned a lot about Jessica Murphy and our other suspects, but we needed more information, so we would have the upper hand. I just wish I had done it before we talked to the good professor and Sam Reece, but with worrying so much about Rembrandt I didn't get around to doing it until last night."

"Doing what?" asked Ryan. "Or do I want to know?"

Megan mulled over his question. "Probably not."

"Tell me anyway. Whatever you're doing can't be any more dangerous than chasing a killer who offers free burial plots to his victims."

"Checking out these people on the Internet," said Megan, fidgeting with her skirt, a long, ankle-length, pleated one, topped with a sleeveless, white silk blouse. She wished she could have worn her work boots, cutoffs, and a red T-shirt emblazoned with the logo of the University of Texas crew team. Megan sighed. She missed crewing. It was an activity that took the edge off her energy, and she needed to get rid of some of her energy or she would be too impatient and push too hard interrogating these suspects.

"The Internet? How will the Internet help find a murderer?"

"I entered the names of all the suspects and read all the interesting secrets that I would bet most of them don't know are available to anyone with an Internet connection. Professor Ryland, for instance, was arrested on Amarillo

Boulevard after he attempted to arrange a little work for hire involving an Asian girl and a vibrating bed in a hot-sheet hotel. The professor seems to prefer Asian girls, must have something to do with his fixation on oriental porcelain. Our member of the bar had his licence to practice law suspended for two years, during which suspension he worked for a brokerage firm in Houston handling retirement funds for energy companies. Can you spell Enron? Let's see, what else? Oh, yes, Anita Reece under went treatment in a private hospital for depression and anxiety, ninety days worth of treatment. She entered the hospital just before Thanksgiving five years ago, just after Jessica Murphy disappeared. Oddly enough, the only honest one of the bunch, is William 'Good Deal Bill' Owens. So much for stereotypes of used car salesmen." She heard Ryan addressing his maker.

"Oh, my God. Oh, my God."

Megan chewed her thumbnail for a moment as she thought. "Let's see, who have I forgotten? Oh, yes, Peggy Otlander. The only thing I could find about her was a short bio. Did you know she took your seminar on Custer? Anyway, I found out how her husband died. It's always a good idea to learn the spouse's cause of death if your suspect is a widow or widower—to make certain that murder isn't a pattern of behavior."

"Oh, my God!" Ryan repeated quietly.

"Her husband died of an overpowering infection that eventually affected the heart muscle. He had Type II diabetes and apparently was unable to fight off the infection."

"Good God, Megan, you're invading our suspects' privacy."

"No, I'm not. I didn't put the information on the Internet, I only accessed it." She wasn't absolutely sure of her legal grounds for her denial, but she figured their suspects would be too busy worrying about staying out of state facilities that featured bars on the windows to be concerned about what secrets the Internet revealed.

"Just where on the Internet did you find that information about Dr. Norman Ryland?"

Megan noticed the fence posts whipping past the passenger window in a blur and looked at the speedometer. "Ryan, slow down! This isn't the Indy 500."

Ryan uttered an expletive and lifted his foot off the gas pedal. "As if you had a right to criticize. You'd challenge Richard Petty. Besides, you're just clutching at any subject to avoid answering my questions. You can't fool me anymore, Megan. I recognize when you're being evasive, and I won't let you get away with it. Tell me, or so help me, I'll turn this truck around and go back to Amarillo and rat you out to Jerry Carr."

Megan glared at him. "The police keep records of arrests, Ryan."

Ryan slammed on the brakes, pulled off the road, and shifted into PARK. He twisted around in the seat to glare at her. "Megan, tell me you didn't hack into the police computer files."

Megan fidgeted with her skirt again, avoiding his eyes. "There are lots of places on the Internet to find information about people. It isn't necessary to hack into protected records."

Ryan straightened around and rested his head against the steering wheel. "You hacked into the police files. You'll be wearing chains and I'll only get to see you on visitors' days."

"My mother offered to do it for me, but she has such a criminal record from being arrested at all the demonstrations she organized, that she would never receive probation, while I have no criminal record at all, so I would be eligible for probation." Her voice trailed off and she flinched at the sight of Ryan's face.

He scooted over on the bench seat, cupped her face in his hands, and stared into her eyes. "If you ever endanger your liberty and your career again, I will kidnap you and lock you in my basement during the day to keep you safe. And at night I will handcuff you to my bed."

"Ryan, I didn't know you had these fantasies about me."

"Shut up! Then I would go on the Internet and e-mail every group your mother ever supported and tell them that she had taken a job writing press releases for the Department of Energy supporting plutonium production facilities in every state; that every vacation she camped in a different national forest, dropping candy wrappers, and chopping down old-growth trees to build campfires; and that she taught courses at night on how to do insider trading without getting caught. How dare she endanger your life and liberty! You can figure out how to get into trouble without her help."

"Ryan! My mother's reputation would be ruined! Green Peace would put out a contract on her." Megan squirmed and pushed against his chest, but she might just as well have pushed a concrete embankment. In fact, an embankment might move sooner.

His pupils dilated and his breath seemed to catch. When he spoke, his voice was husky. "Megan, promise me you won't do anything like this again."

"Ryan!"

"Promise me!"

She debated with herself. She had never lied to Ryan. Evaded, equivocated, exaggerated, but never lied. "I promise I won't ever do anything like that again."

"I'll hold you to your word, Megan."

"You're always yelling at me for getting involved in murder cases and how dangerous it is. I would think you would worry more about our suspects stalking me with a sharp knife than going over the top about a little hacking."

Ryan released her, scooted back over to his side of the truck, and gripped the steering wheel so hard his knuckles turned white. He stared through the windshield in silence.

Megan swallowed and reached over to touch his arm. His muscles were rigid with tension. "Ryan, talk to me. Tell me what I've done that's so wrong. Tell me how I've hurt you."

He turned his head and studied her face, then let go of the steering wheel to stroke her cheek. "You drive me crazy, Megan, with your recklessness. My gut aches every time you're out of my sight. I'm afraid that one of these days one of the killers you persist in challenging will snuff out your life like a candle. I got a permit to carry a concealed weapon just so I can protect you. And I feel pretty good about it. It's one on one, me against the killer, and I figure I've got a better than average chance to take him out before he hurts you. Short of really chaining you to my bed, acting as your bodyguard is the best I can do. But white collar crime—federal crime—I'm helpless to protect you because it's not just one individual after you. Ironic, isn't it? I'm competent to protect you against the bad guys, but I'm no help at all against the good guys."

He fastened his seat belt and drove the rest of the way to the Reeces' adobe-style house. Before they climbed out of the truck Ryan caught her hand. "Megan, how did you find out about Sam Reece?"

"I called the Bar Association. A suspension of a law licence is a public record."

He sighed as he caught her around the waist and lifted her out of the pickup. "Thank God. I could see Sam Reece filing a lawsuit against you."

"I don't think Sam Reece would want Call Me Herb talking about his suspended licence in open court, do you?" She rang the Reece's doorbell.

Anita Reece would have been a beautiful woman if her face had any animation. A strawberry blonde with large, but dull brown eyes, whom Megan estimated to be in her late thirties, Anita Reece was tall with slightly rounded shoulders. She spoke slowly in a monotone, while at the same time she tapped her fingers on the padded arm of her chair in a tuneless repetition of sound. Megan doubted that the woman's medication was the correct dosage.

Even more noticeable than Anita Reece's mental condition and the eye-watering fog of cigarette smoke that floated to the ceiling like a cloud of noxious fumes, was a huge wall display of knives of every size, description, and material mounted on red velvet panels hung from brass rods. From an Aztec sacrificial blade made of volcanic glass, to a prison inmate's shiv made from a stainless steel spoon, the collection exemplified the often ignored relationship between weapons and beauty. A kitchen knife will kill, but a dagger made of the finest steel polished to a sun-reflecting gleam set into a golden hilt topped by a jeweled pommel is not only lethal, but designed to evoke aesthetic appreciation. The blades glittered in the sunlight that poured through a glass door like liquid gold.

"My God, I'm stunned," said Megan, unable to look away from the display. "Every country and culture and historical period in the world must be represented on that wall. I've never seen such a collection outside of a museum."

Mrs. Reece kept swinging her head between Megan and the wall of knives, a confused expression on her face, as if she knew Megan's knowing about the knives was dangerous knowledge, but she wasn't sure for whom it was dangerous. "Sam collects knives," she said in that monotone that lent inexplicable drama to her understatement.

Megan wondered how safe a woman suffering an obvious mental illness would be in a roomful of knives. What was her potential for inflicting injury on herself or someone else? What kind of crisis drove her to a mental institution? What stressor broke her mind, and did her doctors fix it? More important, what did she remember about the disappearance of Jessica Murphy?

Anita Reece scooted forward in her chair until she sat on its very edge. Her fingers were still. She waited, still and silent as a patient in a coma. Megan sensed that without outside stimulus, Anita might sit quietly forever, locked in the hell that was her own mind.

Megan took one last glance at the wall of knives and nudging a spellbound Ryan, sat on the couch. She cleared her throat, and Mrs. Reece took that as a signal to speak.

"I don't understand why you're asking questions about Jessica Murphy. Someone found her skeleton by Indian Rock, so she's not lost anymore." Anita Reece lit a cigarette and inhaled deeply. She seemed calm. At least she had stopped tapping her fingers.

"How did you know I've been asking questions about Jessica Murphy, Mrs. Reece? Dr. Ryan and I haven't mentioned her name to you," said Megan.

Anita Reece rocked back and forth in her chair, her expression that of a woman struggling to remember. "I think Peggy Otlander told me, and I watched you dig her up until Sam told me to come in the house. He likes me to watch happy things. But that was a happy thing because now Jessica isn't lost and you don't need to ask questions anymore."

"Damn Peggy Otlander's big mouth! May she catch laryngitis and lose her voice," muttered Megan under her breath. She heard Ryan chuckle and glared at him.

"It takes one to know one," said Ryan, barely moving his lips to whisper.

Megan clenched her teeth. He was trying to provoke her

by quoting his deadly homily. There was no similarity between her interviews and Peggy Otlander's gossip. Peggy's behavior amounted to interference in a police investigation.

"Yes, I found Jessica, but someone murdered her, Mrs. Reece. We must find out who it is, and I have to ask questions to hear answers," said Megan gently.

"Nobody here killed her," said Anita Reece. She tapped her fingers again, and her voice took on the color of emotion. "Nobody here killed her," she repeated in a louder voice.

"I understand that you and your husband had an angry quarrel over Jessica Murphy? Something about your husband's hiking with Jessica?"

Her fingers began tapping faster, and she shook her head. "I don't know what you're talking about. My husband and I never argue."

"Mrs. Reece, everyone heard you and they still remember five years later, so you can't deny it." Megan wondered if this woman was would shatter before she talked.

Mrs. Reece got up to get an ashtray. A gray crust of ashes covered the bottom, the sign of a heavy smoker and one too depressed to wash her ashtray. She lit one cigarette from the stub of another. She inhaled the smoke deeply, held it, and slowly exhaled. Watching her chain-smoke, Megan decided that Sam Reece must make a sizeable sum every month just to be financially able to keep his wife in cigarettes. She heard Ryan coughing. He was allergic to cigarette smoke, and he would be choked up for days after being exposed to this much smoke. //

"Did you understand me, Mrs. Reece?" asked Megan in as quiet and calm voice as she could manage. It wouldn't do to express any kind of emotion. Questioning Mrs. Reece was like walking across a frozen pond that might crack into chunks of ice under too much weight. The problem was knowing how much weight—or in this case, how much pressure would this woman endure before cracking. ‖

"I suffer from severe depression for which I take a purple pill and a blue pill. I'm not retarded, Dr. Clark. I understand that you're looking for a murderer, and I've already told you that there is no murderer here." Her eyes were no longer dull, but flashing with a manic fire.

"I appreciate your denial of guilt—"

"And I deny Sam's guilt, too," Mrs. Reece interrupted. "Sam didn't kill her. It was her husband."

"No, Mrs. Reece, it's not Gray Wolf Murphy," said Megan in a quiet voice, crossing her fingers behind her back and hoping that she hadn't just told a lie to a sick woman.

Mrs. Reece leaned forward in her chair, a flush coloring her pale face. "It's not my husband; it's one of her other men. Ask that teacher who works at the museum, or the used car dealer who lives across the street. There may be others but I don't know their names."

"Megan, that's enough," said Ryan, standing up and offering her a hand. "Mrs. Reece is not feeling well."

Megan fought conflicted impulses: one urging her to leave the pitiful wreck of a woman alone and the other pushing her to ask another question, to cross-examine her for the truth. She pushed Ryan aside and stood up to step closer to Mrs. Reece, finally kneeling by her chair. "You said 'it's one of her other men.' The inference is that your husband is also one of her men." ‖

Anita Reece tilted her head as if it was heavy to hold up. "I didn't mean to leave that impression. Sometimes I have a hard time saying what I mean. My husband says it my medication and that I must think of exactly what I want to say before I say it." She began tapping her fingers again as she drew deeply on her cigarette.

Megan clasped the hand with the tapping fingers and gently stroked it. Perhaps it would calm the unhappy woman. "Was he having an affair with Jessica Murphy, Mrs. Reece?"

Anita Reece began rocking back and forth. Megan felt the woman's hand twitch, then her fingers moved in a repetitive motion as if she were tapping on the chair arm again. "Why are you asking these questions? Did you see them?"

Megan met Anita's eyes and saw desperation and fear, then nothing. It was as if Anita Reece had left the room, leaving behind a woman who was alive only in the sense that a person on a respirator was alive. Anita Reece had retreated into some closet in her mind and locked the door behind her.

She felt Ryan tugging her arm, his voice low but emphatic. "Stop it, Megan. She can't answer you. She doesn't hear you."

Megan twisted out of his grasp and gripped Anita's shoulders. She couldn't stop now. Anita Reece might never come out of that closet if she did. Stimulus. She must use stimulus—emotional stimulus. "And did your husband take a knife from that wall and stab Jessica Murphy until his arm began to tire? And did he finally lay her in a shallow grave below his own home, so he would always have her close by?"

Mrs. Reece burst into hysterical sobbing, jerking away from Megan and sliding out of her chair and pounding the floor with her fists. "Nobody here killed her. Nobody here killed her." She looked up at Megan, her eyes streaming tears. "I told him that she was bad luck, that he should stay away from her. I told him that she had all kinds of men and that he was just one more. He wouldn't listen—and then she disappeared. The police came out to see Gray Wolf and then they came over here to question us. Sam told them that he and Jessica occasionally hiked in the canyon and that I usually went along."

Ryan grasped Megan under her arms and lifted her up. "My God, what have you done? Shut up, Megan! Shut up now!"

Megan struggled against Ryan's grip. "I can't. I have to finish. I have to save her, damn it! Sam lied, didn't he, Mrs. Reece? He and Jessica hiked alone at least twice a week, didn't he? Why did he lie to the police?" she asked.

Mrs. Reece looked up at Megan. "I don't know. I don't know. Wondering finally drove me crazy and Sam and my doctor committed me." She sat up, wrapped her arms around her knees, and began to rock again.

"Ryan, help me lay her on the couch, then bring me a wet washcloth, please." Megan glimpsed the expression of condemnation in his eyes and quickly looked away. "Mrs. Reece, it's all right. We're finished, and you did so well. Here, let me put this pillow under your head. Thank you, Ryan."

"Don't mention it, *mein Herr* Clark," said Ryan, clicking his heels together.

Megan flinched at the cold tone of his voice. "Let me wipe your face with this washcloth Ryan brought me, and you'll feel so much better." Megan fussed over her, finding Kleenex, pouring her a cold soft drink, and covering her with a light, woolen throw when Anita began to shiver.

Megan sat on the edge of the couch next to Anita Reece. The shattered woman held on to Megan's hand like it was a lifeline, squeezing it until Megan was sure she would have bruises in the morning. She took several deep breaths, thinking how angry Ryan was with her. She leaned over Anita. "That's why you had a breakdown five years ago, and that's why you are so heavily medicated today—because you truly don't know the answer."

Tears flooded Anita Reece's eyes and rolled down the sides of her face. "Yes, that's why. I was so miserable knowing that he and Jessica maybe were having an affair, then she disappeared, but things didn't get any better."

"Why do you believe your husband might have killed Jessica Murphy? I can't help you feel better if I don't know."

"My God, Megan! Now you're practicing medicine without a licence. This is not like putting a Band-Aid on a cut finger. This is messing with someone's mind."

Megan ignored Ryan's admonition. She was going to help this woman despite what Ryan thought. "And there was something that shook your faith in Sam, something that you still wonder about today."

Anita held fast to Megan's hand with both of hers and looked at her with pleading eyes. She licked her dry lips. "He was so relieved when she disappeared. He was very, very happy."

"That would make me wonder, too," said Megan. She pulled one of her hands free from Anita's grip, and held it up like a witness taking an oath before testifying. "I will find the answer and tell you, so help me God. Then you will be able to heal."

//

"What you did was irresponsible, Megan. You could have caused permanent mental damage."

"Her refusal to face her doubts was causing her mind to crumble, Ryan. She just went away. Her body was there but she wasn't. As soon as I realized her mind was hiding, I knew I had to shock her into coming back to reality. Don't you understand?"

Ryan ignored her explanation. "Just when I think you're a mature woman, you do something like this. I don't know how much more of your 'the end justifies the means' motto I can take. You're never too sure about the end, but you'll use some crackpot means that could get you several years in prison if you're caught. Good sense and good advice never stops you. You just bull on through."

Megan sat in the pickup with Ryan, listening to his lecture. She kept her head down, playing with the pleats of her skirt and blinking her stinging eyes, determined not to cry. Everything Ryan said was true and right and sensible. It was just wrong in this case.

"Do you have anything to say, Megan? Are you going to refute my thesis?" asked Ryan. "If not, I'm driving us home, and I don't want to see you for several days. I'll have to let my anger settle, then I'll reevaluate this relationship."

"No," said Megan. "Not home. Drive down South Georgia Street to Good Deal Bill's car lot. We need to talk to Bill Owens."

Ryan sighed and turned on the ignition. "That's what I like about you, Megan. I just told you that I'm breaking up our friendship, and you go right ahead with your objectives on this case. Next suspect is William 'Good Deal Bill' Owens, so by God, that's where we'll go. The phrases 'single minded' and 'focused' don't begin to describe you."

A tear dropped on her skirt, leaving a circle of dampness. Not only did her eyes sting with tears, but her throat burned with the attempt to keep the sobs from bursting out. "Please stop, Ryan. You've beaten up on me enough. You've made your opinion of me quite clear. It doesn't matter that I'm right, that I helped that woman. I'm irresponsible, stubborn, not too careful of the lawfulness of my actions, willing to risk the mental health and safety of other people. I am so possessed of bad habits and dishonesty, that you feel you must cast me out of your life in order to sit alone with your Westerns in your house, never coming out except to go to work or to the grocery store. But you'll be safe from the consequences of my risky behavior and bad habits. And you'll be free of my company."

She reached for the box of Kleenex Ryan always kept in his glove compartment. She plucked several tissues from the box, turned her head toward the window, and blotted her eyes. She blew her nose and dropped the tissue in the little plastic bag hanging from one of the knobs on the dash. Even Ryan's pickup was clean and neat and organized. Her pickup was dirty with empty paper cups and boxes from four different hamburger joints. Her dig box was organized but nothing else was. She wondered how two people as different as she and Ryan could be best friends. Not that they were anymore.

"Megan, what were you trying to do back there with Mrs. Reece?" asked Ryan. His voice was soft but it wasn't contrite. She wanted contrite.

She continued looking out the window. "I was searching for the truth and I was searching for justice for Jessica Murphy. I had to know Anita Reece's side of this many-faceted soap opera, so I could either eliminate her or move her name to the top of the list. And I couldn't wait until her mental condition improved to question her. It was obvious that her mental breakdown was tied to Jessica's disappearance in some way, so the main question was what did she know that caused her falling into depression. As it turned out, I offered her peace of mind."

"Megan, do you mind if I have something to look at besides the back of your head."

She turned around to face him. "Here it is!"

"I made you cry, when all you were doing was searching for truth and justice," said Ryan. "There's not much you wouldn't do when you're searching for truth and justice, is there?"

"The need for truth and justice is what separates us not only from the animals, but from the nihilists of the world, Ryan."

He held out his hand and she accepted it. "Your intentions are always good, Megan, but one of these day your recklessness will hurt you or someone you love."

She waited until she had control of herself. "I guess I'll have to depend on you to save me from the consequences of my recklessness."

He turned his head toward her, his eyes sad. "I don't know if I want that responsibility." But he held her hand the rest of the way to talk to Good Deal Bill.

William 'Good Deal Bill' Owens was as far from the cigar-smoking, pot-bellied, 'Have I got a deal for you' stereotype of a used car salesman as one could imagine. Good Deal Bill was tall and slim, fine-featured, with blond hair and blue eyes. He looked a little like Kirk Douglas playing a Viking. After they introduced themselves, Bill hustled them into his office and closed the door. "Now, what is it you're supposed to ask me?"

"Give us your impression of Jessica Murphy," said Megan, plucking her notebook out of her purse.

"She was one fine lady. She's the reason I'm a success today. She kept telling me to start this business, that I'd be a rich man if I was honest and I stood behind what I sold. It doesn't often happen that I have to take back a car or overhaul one, but when I have to, I do it. No arguing, no trying to weasel out of my agreement. I followed her advice and I've never regretted it. I'm just sorry that she never got to see it." His eyes took on a faraway cast as if he looked back in time to greet a wise woman who gave him counsel.

Megan felt a shiver go up her spine as she saw his face lose its serious good nature to reveal beneath it a sadness. "You were in love with her, weren't you?"

Good Deal Bill's face lost its sad look in an instant, and Megan knew he hadn't meant to let them see his grief. He cleared his throat. "She was the finest woman I have ever known, but she wasn't the happiest. She loved life and she loved people and she loved the canyon. And she loved to dance. When that idiot she was married to left town—which he did on a regular basis—we'd go dancing, mostly square dancing since this was before the revival of ballroom dancing. She would have loved that. She didn't love Gray Wolf," he added in a throwaway manner.

"Did she tell you this?" asked Megan, seeing another image of Jessica Murphy gradually take shape and color.

Bill Owens smiled at her. "Never been in love, have you?" His eyes flicked to Ryan with a curious expression.

Megan felt uncomfortable and embarrassed talking about love with a stranger, but never had she believed in the existence of romantic love so much as at this moment. "No, I don't guess I've ever loved anyone—really, I mean."

"I know what you mean," said Bill Owens, a look of sympathy in his eyes. "I never *really* did either until I met her. And to answer your question, Jessica never talked about Gray Wolf except in the most objective terms, sort of the way a man's secretary talks about her boss's schedule. There was never any music in her voice. But she never left home looking for love. She was the kind of a woman who any decent man would feel like he had lied to the preacher if he thought about making a pass. The only time I ever touched her was escorting her to the car or dancing." He looked away again with that same distant expression. "She never told me she didn't love that idiot, Gray Wolf. A man in love just knows."

"Do you know of anyone with a reason to murder Jessica Murphy?" asked Megan.

Bill Owens rubbed his chin and looked thoughtful. "No

man who knew her like I did would kill her, and that includes Norman Ryland and Sam Reece. She'd talk about the professor sometimes, about how he was a lonely man and how she wished she knew a lady his age who liked oriental porcelain. We used to list all the single women we knew looking for a wife for Ryland."

"As for Sam, he just liked to go hiking, one of those outdoor-exercise fanatics. I enjoy hiking mostly to see the animals and the scenery, maybe explore some out-of-the-way canyon branching off the big canyon. I'd go with them a lot of the time, and sometimes Anita would go, too, but she didn't much like it. She'd just go because she was so insecure that she was afraid Sam had something going with Jessica."

"Did they have any kind of relationship?" asked Megan. If Bill Owens was jealous, this was the question that would cause his voice to reveal any anger.

Bill Owens laughed. "Does the woman I've been talking about sound like she would have an affair?"

Megan shook her head. "No, but some women—and men—are wonderful actors. She might have been one."

Bill Owens leaned over his desk to get closer to Megan. "Let me see if I can describe Jessica so you'll understand her. Think of a pool of water deep in a cave somewhere. That water is so pure and so clear that you can see all the way to the bottom, but you try to reach that bottom and you can't because it's several times deeper than it looks. That was Jessica: clean and pure and clear and deep, so deep you might know her for a hundred years and just began to *really* know her. A woman who'd jump into bed with any man who asked would be that same kind of pool except it would be about an inch deep."

"Why do you suppose Sam Reece would be happy and

relieved after Jessica disappeared?" asked Megan, Jessica's image growing clearer and clearer in her mind.

Bill Owens looked shocked for a moment, then rubbed his chin again in what Megan decided must be a habit. "Maybe because it got him out of having to break off his friendship with Jessica which he really dreaded. A lot of people don't like Sam—and I suspect he cuts corners as far as the law is concerned—but when Sam is being honest— which might not be too often—he's honest all the way through. He really enjoyed those hikes we all took together. I think Jessica and I were the only two friends Sam had, everybody else he knows are just acquaintances. You can see how hard it was going to be for Sam. Everybody needs friends, Dr. Clark, even crooked lawyers. So when the whole business took care of itself with Jessica's disappearance, I could see how he'd be relieved. You see, one of the other people—maybe the only other person—that Sam holds close to his heart is his wife. You have to understand about Anita. She's always been about a step away from falling into that black hole she carries around inside herself. Anything gets a little off balance—or she thinks it's off balance—she falls into that black hole and it takes Sam and her psychiatrist and a whole bunch of pills to pull her out. It's not her fault, you understand, her brain is wired cockeyed or maybe has a few loose connections, so life for her is standing around waiting to fall. Well, Sam and Anita had a real big fight one night about Jessica. Anita was jealous and no way can you reason with people like her. She grabs an idea from out of the air and obsesses about it. Sam called me about it the next day frantic about what he was going to have to do. Well, he planned to put an end to the friendship the following Sunday. It never happened because Jessica disappeared. I can see why Sam was relieved. Somebody took the whole business out of his hands. But I can tell you this, that relief didn't last long. If you've seen him, you haven't seen a happy man. It's just him and Anita in the whole world."

"Would he murder Jessica?"

Bill Owens shook his head. "No way, and neither would I nor Norman Ryland. I don't know Gray Wolf Murphy all that well."

Megan rose out of her chair and shook hands with Bill Owens. "Thank you so much. I feel like I know Jessica a lot better now."

Good Deal Bill escorted them out of his office and to Ryan's pickup. The day seemed brighter with a slight breeze that brought up goose bumps on Megan's bare arms. Fall had arrived even if the trees weren't turning, she could see it in the changing light. Each season in the Panhandle had its own kind of light, from the hot blinding white light of summer, to the harsh gray light of the winter. She thought of Jessica Murphy lying in her grave in the Palo Duro while the seasons cycled year after year, and the cotton-wood trees turned bright yellow, and snow fell softly on the wild plum trees. She was sorry all of a sudden that Jessica's grave had been disturbed. Jessica might have liked to spend eternity resting in Palo Duro Canyon.

What about the mummy, the one Megan privately thought of as Miss Comanche, would she like spending eternity in Palo Duro Canyon? Alone? Her Comanche lover was most likely buried in Oklahoma where the Comanche reservation used to be before the land was signed over to the Indians in equal shares of so many acres, and what was left over was opened up to white settlement. Or maybe he died in the Red River War that marked the defeat of the Comanche and their removal to Oklahoma, and he lay in some unmarked grave. Megan knew of no way of learning the lover's name, and without his name finding his grave was impossible. Maybe it would be impossible even if she knew his name. Miss Comanche and her lover must rest apart, and suddenly she felt an almost overwhelming sadness that it should be so.

Bill Owens opened the truck's door for her, but Megan hesitated. There was something, some thought that if she could only recall, some connection if she could only make it, that would be the key that unlocked the mystery of Jessica's death. She thought for a moment longer, then turned to Bill Owens. "Why do you keep calling Gray Wolf an idiot?"

He laughed. "Because he was running around to every Comanche's house, every pow wow, every Indian celebration of any kind trying to make medicine, a kind of spiritual magic, when he had all the magic any man needs right in his own living room."

17

*To me an anomalous fact—a fact which appears un-
connected, or even discordant with the body of known
facts—is precisely the one on which attention should
be focused.*

—Dr. John Thorndyke in R. Austin Freeman's
The Stoneware Monkey, 1938

AMARILLO, TEXAS, PRESENT DAY

Megan sat over on the other side of the pickup, chewing her thumbnail and staring through the windshield. She was silent and had been since we left William
'Good Deal Bill' Owens's car lot. He gave us a lot to think
about, and I had spent some twenty blocks and three stop-
lights thinking. I liked his analogy of the deep pool of water in a cave. Megan is like Jessica: so deep that every time
I think I can predict her actions, thoughts, or behavior, I
find myself in over my head and drowning. She's decep-
tive. One gets too tied up in her petite size and her curly
red hair. She looks so sweet and innocent until the moment
she bites you.

I had been so sure of myself when I lectured her on her
means to her end. She was looking for truth and justice.
That's admirable. The question remains: Is the search for
truth worth any cost, personal or material? Megan would

answer yes. Too many years living with a mother who was a veteran of demonstrations for causes had taught Megan to stake out the high moral ground regardless of the cost to herself or others. At least she isn't sacrificing individuals for spotted owls, but I believe her blind devotion to ideals will cause her many sleepless nights.

"I think Bill Owens is innocent," I said, mostly for something to say although I believed he *was* innocent. Not that it mattered what I thought since Megan had always proved impervious to influence.

"He certainly drew us a different picture of Jessica." Her voice sounded odd, as if she answered me while thinking of something else.

"And of Sam Reece."

She turned her head to look at me. "What do you think of his opinion of Sam Reece? You know him. Do you agree with Bill Owens?"

"He's just an acquaintance, not a friend—"

"I won't fail you if you are wrong," she said, interrupting me, which doesn't often happen.

"Remembering the old adage that there's a little bit of good in everyone, yes, I mostly agree. Even Jesse James loved his wife and family, and Billy the Kid worshiped Tunstall. Or maybe Tunstall was a convenient excuse to run wild with his six-shooter."

"Ryan, you're equivocating. This isn't a multiple-choice test. I don't want options, I want a yes or no answer."

"If those are my only two choices, then I pick yes. I'd hire another attorney to look over any work Sam Reece did for me, but I can believe that he loves his wife—just like Jesse James, and like Jesse, I can see Sam robbing trains in his off-hours."

"I agree. Now, let's go talk to our client, the great shaman, Gray Wolf Murphy."

"What? Why do we need to talk to Gray Wolf?"

"Because we've heard everyone's opinions of Jessica except Gray Wolf's. We heard about her hereditary disorders—if the murderer had waited a few years she would probably have died of natural causes—but we didn't hear anything personal about her. And the way he talked of waiting seven years to have her declared legally dead sounded cold to me, like he was counting down the days until he could meet Peggy Otlander at the altar—" She stopped abruptly, wrinkling her forehead which she always does when she has a revelation.

"What is it? What did you think of? Do you know the murderer?"

She blinked as if she was trying to focus her eyes on my face. "Yes, I think so, but I have to prove it now, and after five years . . . Ryan, how does Gray Wolf live? I mean, what does he live on? Oh, I mean, what kind of a job does he have?"

It was my turn to blink. "I don't know, Megan. I don't know the man, and I've never thought about it."

"Don't you think it's time we do think about it? I'm going to call Herb to meet us at Gray Wolf's." She lifted her cell phone out of her purse. I was surprised she could find it among the confusion of objects she carried in a purse little smaller than a backpack, but maybe the size of the phone made it easier to find. "That's not it, that's my harmonica." She played a few bars of "Old Susanna," grinned at me, dropped it on the seat between us, and dove back into the abyss.

"Megan, my cell phone is in my glove compartment. Use it."

"What's it doing in there?" she asked, retrieving it and punching in some numbers.

"I bought one when you embarked on this dangerous avocation of amateur sleuthing. I want you to be able to get hold of me when you need help wherever I am."

"Even when you're in class?"

"Carry it with me."

She released her seat belt to scoot over and kissed me. On the cheek, damn it. I looped my arm around her shoulders. "Sit by me, honey. This is a bench seat. There's a seat belt in the middle."

She smiled at me. She has a beautiful, heart-melting smile when she uses it. She fastened her seat belt and scooted as close to me as she could get. "What will the neighbors say, Ryan?"

My heart was thundering in my ears. "I only care what one neighbor says. What are you going to say, neighbor?"

Suddenly she straightened up. "Herb, this is Megan. Say, could you meet—" she stopped abruptly and listened, the pink flush that always tinted her cheeks fading away. She wrinkled her forehead, and I had a premonition of a coming predicament.

She dragged her fingers through her hair, tangling her curls even more than they were naturally. She reached over and grabbed my thigh, digging her nails in, which was just as well since the pain settled things down in the immediate region. "Herb, meet us at Indian Rock on the side opposite the rim. We're nearly at the canyon, so no way will Jerry catch us. You lag behind him by a mile or two, so he won't see you head for the canyon. Tell Jerry we're on our way to Gray Wolf's—which technically we are, so you won't be lying to him. Just don't mention to him exactly where at Gray Wolf's we'll be. And Herb, call Gray Wolf on your cell phone and tell him to slide down from the rim and meet us at Indian Rock. There are plenty of juniper to break his fall."

She hung up the phone and looked at me. "Jerry Carr is at Herb's office demanding to know where we are."

The predicament had arrived.

"Megan," I whispered, crouching behind Indian Rock. "We are evading the police. That has to be against the law. We'll both end up at the correction facility, and they'll put me in a cell with Guido, the three-hundred-pound biker with ugly tattoos."

"Ryan, quit whining. We have issues here we need to discuss." She turned toward Gray Wolf. "How's your wrist? You really think it's broken?"

Gray Wolf leaned against the rock holding his arm a few inches above the wrist. It did zig where it should have zagged. "My wrist doesn't hurt as much as my knee. I tore the cartilage when I played high school football, and I think I tore it again. Ruined a good pair of slacks, too."

"What were you doing sliding down a cliff in slacks?" asked Megan. She had that impatient tone in her voice that meant she wanted to get her business done and get out of Dodge before she met Guido's girlfriend.

"I *didn't know* I would be sliding down a cliff," said Gray Wolf in more of a whine than I managed on my best day.

"Please. We should all keep our voices down. Jerry and Special Crimes are in your house as we speak," said Herb in such a soft voice that I could hardly hear him.

"Wait! Why did Jerry bring Special Crimes?" asked Megan.

Herb patted his forehead with a pristine white handkerchief. Herb had been in more predicaments in the seven months or so that he had known Megan than in the whole of his previous lifetime. "Jerry has a search warrant. He will be looking for human blood using Luminol, and knives of the approximate size and shape you estimated the murder weapon to be."

Gray Wolf hunched over and put his head in his hands. "Oh, no! I have a whole wall full of knives. I collect knives. Most of them are Comanche flint blades, but I have others. I'll be in limbo for weeks or months because those are bound to have blood on them, and some of it will be human."

"Damnation!" said Megan. "Did you notice any of your knives missing around the time of Jessica's disappearance?"

"No, and I'm very familiar with my collection. And there were no gaps where a knife should be hanging. You know, Megan, if we could hurry along? My knee is about to kill me."

"Pretend you're a Comanche warrior riding into the canyon from a raid with a bullet in your shoulder and one in your calf. You can't make a sound because warriors don't moan about their wounds. Use your imagination." Megan wrinkled her forehead and thought. "I might as well ask my questions so Herb can take him to the hospital. Where's your insurance card, Gray Wolf?"

"Inside in my wallet. But it doesn't matter. I'll pay cash for tonight, then Herb, if you could bring my card by the hospital tomorrow? After the lieutenant takes my knife collection—"

"And he finds evidence of blood somewhere in your house, but probably in your living room," said Megan, sounding as gloomy as she does every time she applies to work on some ghastly corpse and is passed over.

"What blood?" demanded Gray Wolf in a squeaky voice.

"I think Jessica was murdered in your house, then dragged out to your balcony and tipped over the edge. Your house is directly above Indian Rock. No one would see the murderer with a dead body if it was dark."

"Oh, God!" exclaimed Gray Wolf.

Three voices shushed him. Megan looked at him. "What kind of job do you have that you earn enough to pay cash for a hospital visit?"

"That's private."

"You may be lying in a hospital room with an armed guard outside the door by this time tomorrow, Gray Wolf. You may be charged with murder at any moment. You have no privacy! Herb is your lawyer, and Ryan and I are your investigators. Anything you tell us is confidential. I need to know so I can eliminate you from contention as murderer of the year."

"I have some money invested from a settlement when I was in a car wreck. I've got enough to pay for a visit to the emergency room. My insurance company will reimburse me. And I usually get a little honorarium when I bless a house or speak about medical treatments of the Comanche. I make out, but I'm not rich."

I couldn't stand it. "The Nermernuh did not have shamans who blessed houses. There were medicine men who treated the sick, but not shamans. If they have one now it is because their culture has been polluted by that of other Plains tribes, which is a damn shame, because the Nermernuh were a tremendously interesting culture. They were a hunter-gatherer horse Indian culture in its purest form. They lived by the code of the warrior and many of their young men died by it. I hate to see their culture amalgamated into a generic being called the Plains Indian. That wasn't a tribe; it was a white Easterner's image of the Indian, created by Buffalo Bill's Wild West Show and nurtured by movies and television since."

Megan put her hand over my mouth. "Ryan, you're on a soapbox again, and you're raising your voice."

"Sorry. I obsess sometimes on Indian culture."

"You're probably right in everything you say, Dr. Stevens, but the Comanche culture as you describe is gone. It was gone the minute Quanah Parker, war chief of the last free band, surrendered and stepped on the reservation for the first time, because the Comanche culture depended on a free, unfettered life with buffalo to eat and someone to fight. What we have left is sadness for what we lost, and the recognition of the inevitability of evolving into the white man's idea of the Plains Indian. It's not much, but we cling to it."

"You mean they evolved from the Nermernuh, as they identified themselves, into the Comanche, which is how the white identifies them," I said. I was becoming as gloomy as Megan.

"Are you Comanche at all?" asked Megan, looking at his red hair.

He flushed red enough to hide his freckles. "I'm one sixty-fourth. I always tell my audiences that what little Comanche blood I have is safe in my heart. They seem to accept that."

"Ryan sidetracked us for a few minutes, but I still need some answers. What dates were you gone when Jessica disappeared?"

"I was in Oklahoma from the twentieth of September to the twenty-third. I came home the evening of the twenty-third to find Jessica gone. I waited until the next afternoon, the twenty-fourth, to report her missing."

"So Jessica could have been murdered anytime between the late morning of the twentieth to the late afternoon of the twenty-third. We have no way of knowing exactly when she died, so there's no way to establish alibis." She ran her fingers through her curls which immediately sprang back to their former tangles. "One more question, Gray Wolf, and you can go to the hospital, and Ryan and I will go see if Jerry plans to introduce us tonight to Guido, the three-hundred-pound biker, and his body-pierced girlfriend. Now, please describe Jessica for me."

Gray Wolf looked surprised. "Well, she was about five feet, seven inches, and she had brown hair with a red cast to it, and gray eyes. She's the only person I've ever met who had real gray eyes."

"No, I mean personal impressions, not physical details. I can get those from a picture," said Megan.

Gray Wolf sat without speaking for a few minutes. "I don't have a picture. That was the only thing that was missing along with Jessica. Every photograph I had of her was gone. I used to carry one in my wallet, but it was stolen about six months after Jessica disappeared."

"Did you report that to the police when you reported Jessica's disappearance?" I asked. The hair on the back of my neck stood up. Those stolen pictures were the most frightening fact of this murder. A knife is considered a very up-close and personal weapon, but the theft of the pictures seemed a curse on Jessica. Sure enough, she didn't rest easy in her grave.

Gray Wolf cleared his throat and looked over his shoulder. I felt like doing the same thing, and it wasn't even dark yet. Megan moved over to sit by me. Our shoulders touched and I held tight to her hand. If there were ghosts here, Megan had handled their earthly remains with respect. She would be safe at Indian Rock, but no one wants to visit with ghosts at night. As for myself, in about three hours when the sun sank far enough in the west to fill the canyon with shadows, you couldn't pay me to stay in the Palo Duro or anywhere near Indian Rock.

"Jessica was a lady in the old southern tradition," said Gray Wolf. "She was soft-spoken, kind, kept the house beautifully, and was a wonderful cook. She was a gracious hostess for a man who never wanted any parties. She had a wide range of general knowledge, certainly more than I have, so she could have a conversation with anyone. You know how at a casual party in this part of the world, the women will stand in the kitchen talking, or in a corner of the living room, while the men will stand in a different place. Jessica was always with the men because she said our conversation was more interesting. You wouldn't call her a man's woman though. She was her own woman and that made her special and men admired her. Dr. Ryland at the museum thought she walked on water, and not just because she liked Chinese porcelain. Dr. Ryland has a few problems and Jessica would listen to him. She said at first he would act like a dictatorial museum curator, knew everything about every exhibit when he didn't, overbearing to the staff. Finally, he dropped the act and just talked to her. I don't know if he was in love with her or not, but I think he was. I wasn't worried. He was afraid to make a pass, and she would have quit her museum job if he had."

"She loved to go hiking in the canyon with Sam Reece and Bill Owens. I never worried about Sam. He is crazy for his wife, which is unexpected for a cold-as-ice lawyer. Bill was in love with Jessica, about as much in love as any man I ever met. Jessica should have married him instead of me."

"Did you love your wife, Gray Wolf?" asked Megan softly.

"She wanted to go home to Kentucky where there were trees and babbling brooks and green pastures and all the other stereotypes she talked about. The only thing she loved in this part of the country was Palo Duro Canyon. She would sit for hours on the balcony watching the canyon change with the seasons. She though I was deluding myself acting the part of the shaman, so she never went with me. We just drew apart and found one day that we were strangers sleeping in the same bed. Jessica moved into the guest room the summer before she disappeared. We never talked about it; she just moved. That's when I knew the marriage was over. The problem was I loved what she was but not who she was. I didn't know who she was at all."

18

They say murder is grave because irrevocable, be-
cause you can't bring life back. Are the crimes not
graver when, and because, life goes on? When the
consequences continue to ripple steadily outward . . .
distorting and destroying?

—Nicholas Freeling's *Arlette,* 1981

PALO DURO CANYON, 1868

"Buffalo Woman, I see your father walking up the canyon.
You'd better go get him. He is too blind and too old to be
walking by himself. If he falls and breaks his leg or his
arm, he is too old to heal quickly," said Spotted Tongue.
"The old die in much pain from their many parts. If you
save your father from further pain, I believe it would in-
crease your honor for others."

Buffalo Woman stood up and peered down the canyon.
"If my father can't keep up with the Nermernuh, then he
will give away his ponies and stay behind and go east beyond the sun. I will leave my mother with him for she can't
manage without him. If the Tejanos come, she can't see to
escape. She can't find her pony or ride it. She must ride
with someone else which puts another Nerm in danger.

Spotted Tongue would rather have faced a band of Tejanos more numerous than all the Nermernuh than hear

Buffalo Woman's words. How do you cut your heart in two by leaving your parents to die?

"Don't look so at me, Spotted Tongue. Many winters ago there was a custom that my father's grandfather told him about, a story that my father's grandfather had heard from his own grandfather, so see, Spotted Tongue, the story is very old. In this custom the old who could not keep up, whose teeth were gone and could not chew the skins to soften them, these old people would walk away from the camp and not return. They would walk away to die. They would do it for the good of the Nermernuh."

Spotted Tongue understood what was good about the custom for the Nermernuh, but it was bad for them, too. The old walking away to die while the Nermernuh watched repulsed him. The distance between murder and suicide was very short, and Spotted Tongue thought that any death of a Nerm that the Nermernuh stood by and watched happen without interfering made the People less honorable. Spotted Tongue decided it was a bad custom when there was plenty to eat. He didn't like the way Buffalo Woman talked about the custom, as if she would follow it when she tired of caring for her parents.

"That is not the custom among the Nermernuh now, so go take care of your father." He watched her leave, but her walk was stiff and angry. Maybe he wouldn't take Buffalo Woman for his second wife after all.

He turned to Green Willow. "You said to learn the why of Little Flower's murder. That was good counsel. So I will ask myself what each warrior and each woman will gain. I will take Fat Belly first. What had he to gain? If he used Little Flower, it would break our friendship, but his use of her would make us brothers as two men who use the same woman become. He would pay ponies and perhaps his knife that is the color of grass. Yes, I would demand that knife. No one else among the Nermernuh has a knife like that. But Fat Belly might not want to pay with his ponies and knife, so would he murder Little Flower? No, I do not believe it, Green Willow. How does this story feel to you? Does your belly tell you it is truth or a lie?"

Green Willow laid aside the deerskin covered with plums, and Spotted Tongue let the peace of the canyon sooth his grief while he waited for her to speak. The shadows gathered around the camp now that the sun had disappeared below the canyon's rim. The shadows gave its color to the evening air, turning it to a soft gray mist that touched the skin but did not leave water drops as a real mist would. When the great Mother Moon rose in the east the air would turn silver with its light. Soon Green Willow would build the cook fire and the smell of roasting buffalo smeared with crushed plums and pierced by nuts would add flavor to the color of the air. Spotted Tongue's heart swelled with love for the Nermernuh and the comfort of life that remained unchanged. But for how long? He grew uneasy. He had seen the Tejanos's camps of wooden tipis growing larger, and now the Nermernuh must jump their ponies over the fences built of hard gray rope with sharp points that ripped the bellies out of ponies who could not jump high enough. And he had pondered the meaning of the long, black iron horse whose belly carried the Tejanos from one camp to another faster than a horse could run. The Nermernuh must keep the land they controlled from the Tejanos.

But there so many Tejanos and also the Americans who looked like the Tejanos but were not, and the Mexicans who hated the Nermernuh. We are few, he thought, and they are so many. We must be more fierce than those white men. We must raid and take many scalps to warn the white men to recognize the land we already control is ours. We must fight to live the way of the People.

"Spotted Tongue! Do you hear me or have the fights of today made you deaf?" asked Green Willow in a loud voice.

Spotted Tongue smiled at Green Willow's concerned face. "I was thinking of the air and smelling the buffalo cooking and asking the Father Sun that the way of the People not change for our lives and our children's lives and our children's children as long as there is a Nerm standing on this land."

Green Willow smiled and touched his chest, caressing the suddenly tender skin. "You think thoughts like a very old shaman whose medicine is strong. I think I like you better showing off on your pony, shouting and laughing after a raid. You are not so different then."

Spotted Tongue grew cold with dread. "You think I am different? How am I different now?"

"I don't know the words to tell you. I think there aren't any words. You are a Nerm, but sometimes the look in your eyes is the same as the look in Little Flower's eyes, like you stand far away and look at the rest of us. It scares us, all of us. There is something that has changed you, or maybe you changed yourself." She shook her head and threw out her arms, angry at not knowing more words. Spotted Tongue didn't know the words, either.

Green Willow smiled and acted a little unsure of herself, then straightened her shoulders and looked into his eyes. "Now, you asked me what my belly says about Fat Belly. He did not kill Little Flower and our child. My belly tells me so. He has more to lose than to gain. You would take many of his ponies, and maybe his arrows so you wouldn't have to make any when the snow flies. And what would he gain? The use of Little Flower? She was beautiful, more beautiful than any Nerm, but I don't think Fat Belly would risk so much for a moment's pleasure. Slow Like a Turtle is also beautiful and loves Fat Belly and moves beneath him until he feels his head will come off. She told me so. But if Fat Belly uses Little Flower, then his own woman will go away in her mind whenever he touches her. But more than loss and gain, Fat Belly is innocent because he loves you like a brother, loves you too much to use your woman."

Spotted Tongue nodded his head and decided that a smart women is worth many ponies, maybe all the ponies a man has but one. "So let's weigh Shaking Hand. He has a pretty woman who is smarter than Wild Horse's wife. Topay is a hard worker, and I believe she gives Shaking Hand much pleasure in their robes at night. So why would he use Little Flower when he already has a good wife? And if he used Little Flower, he would have to pay me many ponies and whatever else he has that I want. And Topay would cool toward him. Thus Shaking Hand is innocent. What do you say, woman? Let your belly speak."

Green Willow gathered a handful of small sticks and leaves and arranged them within the ring of rocks that marked their cook fire. Spotted Tongue laid on his side watching her. He wanted to urge her to speak, but it was impolite to interrupt someone who is speaking, even if they just hesitate to think. "It is as you say, Spotted Tongue. Shaking Hand is true to his friendship."

Spotted Tongue sat up. His good mood left him as he considered his last friend. "Next is Wild Horse. My reasoning for him is the same as Fat Belly and Shaking Hand. He has more to lose than to gain. I would say that he was happy with his woman, but I don't think that is true. Deer Fawn complains at every breath. But there are many unmarried women in camp and many captive women if he needs one to share his robes at night, or if he wants a second wife. He hasn't done that yet. I would almost say, Green Willow, that if Little Flower were still alive, he would take her now to relieve his anger at me. He drew his knife on me, did you know that? What does your belly say about that?"

Green Willow turned away from her task of building a fire to stare at Spotted Tongue in fear. "Will you ask the council to let you and Wild Horse fight to the death? Can you mend your friendship?"

"I will not fight him, Green Willow. I would be his friend, and I think once his son is born, he will be more of the Wild Horse of old. And I think he's innocent. I don't believe that his wife had anything to with Little Flower's murder. She's too big with Wild Horse's son."

Green Willow shook her head and laughed, but her laughter had no pleasure in it "You men! So sure the child she carries is a son. But don't trust that the birth will restore Wild Horse as he was last winter. When we move camp to hunt the buffalo, and Deer Fawn has to ride horseback, her labor will start. You men have no idea how miserable riding a horse is when you're in labor. But too often you cannot stop to wait for us. Often there is too much danger. But too many of our women lose their babies from living on horseback like we do. And too many of our women deliver early like Deer Fawn will do. You men wonder why so many tipis are empty of children's voices. It is because too many of our women lose their babies almost before they know they are carrying new life. It may be that Wild Horse's son, if it is a son, will not live. How will Wild Horse act if that happens, as it most likely will? He will look to empty his anger. And who is he angry with now? You, Spotted Tongue. His anger with you may carry over."

Spotted Tongue heard the wisdom of Green Willow's words, but wanted to hang onto his trust that in the end Wild Horse would follow the way of the People. "I will think on your words, but hope that they prove false."

"I hope that, too, Spotted Tongue, but some things will never change. Again, however Wild Horse feels now, he would not have broken the tie between you to kill Little Flower. But of all your friends, Wild Horse is the one who worries me most. He carries a grudge."

Spotted Tongue stood up and began to pace in front of the arbor. "All we have proven is that nobody killed Little Flower." He felt his grief cover him up again.

"But there are the women, Spotted Tongue. Don't forget the women."

"All right. Deer Fawn is too big carrying Wild Horse's son. Slow Like a Turtle walks with Deer Fawn, so the two of them would support one another's stories. You left first and you were alone and innocent. You could not turn back on the path without being seen by those behind you."

"Not that I felt like a sister to her, Spotted Tongue. Most of the time I hated her, but I didn't kill Little Flower. But the reason I didn't kill has nothing to do with hate. I did not kill her because I love you. I knew her death would change you forever. You will always wear a robe of grief. How much more would you grieve if it had been I who killed her?"

Spotted Tongue was a long time speaking, but not because he was touched by Green Willow's words. He hardly heard them. Buffalo Woman walked by him with her father and spoke to him, but her words might as well have been flies buzzing in his ears for he didn't hear her words, either. There was something about Little Flower's murder that would answer many questions, and if he used his different way of thinking, the how of her murder would be clear.

Still thinking, he carried on with the loss or gain of the women. "Slow Like a Turtle is innocent. I will not consider that she would kill Little Flower. She was the only woman in camp who liked her and could talk to her. No, Slow Like *a Turtle is innocent. She could come to me and say 'I killed Little Flower,' and I still would believe her innocent. And what does your belly say?"*

"Innocent, of course," said Green Willow, crushing the plums to go on top of the buffalo. Spotted Tongue noticed that she was using the cook pan, the fri pan that Little Flower wanted.

"Next woman is Topay, Shaking Hand's wife."

"I know whose wife she is, Spotted Tongue. We do many tasks together, from picking plums to gathering dried buffalo dung for cook fires. She makes me laugh."

"I don't know her well, but she didn't mind answering my questions when I could get her to talk about Little Flower and picking plums instead of Deer Fawn. She was talking . . ." Spotted Tongue fell silent as he recalled bits of his conversation with Topay. If he was right, the how of the murder was clear before him. As for the why, he knew because Green Willow told him. He didn't believe it at first and blundered around making his friends angry. He believed it now. "I have to go talk to Topay again."

Green Willow stood by the cook fire, rocking back and forth with her hands covering her face. "It's Topay, isn't it, Spotted Tongue? I have to mourn the woman she used to be."

Spotted Tongue hugged Green Willow, but gently so his ribs hurt but a little. "Think of the only one who would gain by killing Little Flower, but the gain rested on a gamble that was as uncertain as Fat Belly winning at dice. Like Fat Belly, the murderer lost. Little Flower's death gained her murderer nothing."

The shadows gathering around the camp were dark now. Some were black where the trees added their shade to the shadows. Cook fires added their yellow and red flames to the night, but the Great Mother Moon had yet to rise. This end of the camp was the darkest because of the cottonwood trees adding their shade. Suddenly Spotted Tongue shivered and bumps rose on his skin. He turned back to call to his first wife. "Green Willow, will you be all right? It is very dark and you are alone."

"Go, my husband. I am not a child to be scared of the dark." He felt her watching him as he walked toward Shaking Hand's arbor. He felt the air from another body as he walked through a black shadow. He turned, but was too slow. The knife went into his back.

A voice whispered as he crumbled first to his knees, then his belly. "The spirit of the white Cannibal Owl as a woman captured you. You are cursed." He felt the light on his head and shoulders, but the rest of his body lay in the black shadows. He heard Green Willow screaming as his mind followed his body into the black shadows.

19

From any crime to its author there is a trail. It may be . . . obscure, but, since matter cannot move without disturbing other matter along its path, there always is—there must be—a trail of some sort. And finding and following such trails is what a detective is paid to do.

—"House Dick" in Dashiell Hammett's
Dead Yellow Women, 1947

AMARILLO, TEXAS, PRESENT DAY

Agnes Caldwell slapped her hands together. "Everyone get a cup of coffee or a soft drink if you want, and one of Lorene's Toll House cookies, and we'll be ready to start. Megan, I hope you have a really interesting report with lots of detail."

"Yes." said Randel Anderson, standing up, which the club agreed didn't add to the intimacy of the group, so Megan knew he did it just to be obstinate. She noticed that he was wearing a pair of beige jeans with an actual crease. She didn't think she had seen a pair of jeans with a crease since grade school. That must be why he stood up, to show off his crease.

Randel continued, stroking his goatee which no longer resembled a goat's, thanks to Candi Hobbs' influence. "We

haven't heard a word from you since you dug up Miss Comanche, with the help of Murder by the Yard Reading Circle I might add. So get to it, old girl." He tugged on his
crease before he sat down.

"Do bring us up to date, Megan," said Rosemary Pittman,
her voice sounding a little reproachful. "Personally, I've felt
so useless this week, and the first twenty-four hours are the
most important in any murder case. After that the trail gets
cold."

"Rosemary, the case is five years old! I don't think the
twenty-four hour rule applies," said Megan, amused at the
white-haired lady.

Megan might as well not have wasted her time defending herself, as Rosemary went on talking as if she hadn't
heard Megan. "And Lorene has felt frustrated, haven't you,
Lorene?"

Lorene Getz, who was sitting on one side of retired Lieutenant Ray Roberts while Rosemary sat on the other side,
backed up her friend. "That's right, Megan. I had Rosemary
and Ray over to my house for a light supper this week, and
we kicked around, is that the correct term, Ray? the case, but
without more clues we couldn't begin to deduce the perp."
She sounded a little miffed.

Megan had noticed that Lorene and Rosemary both had
begun sprinkling police jargon in their speech. Without
doubt the influence of Ray Roberts. "There wasn't much to
report until today. I mean, I had a list of suspects, but I
didn't know enough about them except cold first impressions. I know more now."

"I really think you should have told us who the suspects
were before tonight, Megan," said Candi Hobbs. Candi was
anal retentive, the kind of person who memorized the copyright date of every mystery she read, studied, or heard of.

Megan was getting tired of being criticized. "Look,

there wasn't a lot for you to do. You couldn't help me with the autopsies, and there was no need for any of you to research the suspects since I found the preliminary information on the Internet. I didn't want to ask any of you to do that because I obtained some of the information in an unorthodox way."

"What did you do, Megan? Hack into the police files?" Randel asked, slapping his knee and laughing like a hyena.

"The security on the police department's computer system is worthless," said Ray. "My five-year-old grandson could probably hack into it."

Megan felt her face turning red. "I never said I hacked into police files. Stop putting words in my mouth. There are numerous ways to retrieve information from the Internet that are perfectly legal."

Megan could feel Ryan's eyes boring through the back of her skull and tried to swallow a knot in her throat. She hadn't lied yet but she might have to if Randel didn't shut up. She didn't want anyone in Murder by the Yard to know of her computer crime—if it was a crime. Were police reports public records or not? She didn't know.

"Still," said Agnes with a frown of disapproval. "You should have told us, Megan. We did agree at the time of our very first case that we were partners in investigating any crime. I think you have forgotten that."

Megan held down her rising temper. "I apologize, everyone. Does anyone else want to pull on their boots and walk all over me? If not, I'll give my report with a list of the suspects."

Ryan stood up, looking taller, stronger, and meaner than Megan had ever seen him. "Everybody back off. Megan has busted her butt this week trying to put together a thumbnail sketch of the assorted suspects, and getting all that information together so you'd have something to work with hasn't been easy. I also want everybody to remember that Megan is point man in this investigation, and that means if someone thinks we're getting too close to the solution to this puzzle, she will be the first one to die. Someone has been fat and happy and proud of himself or herself for getting away with murder for *five* years. Then here comes Megan and Murder by the Yard putting the fear of God or life in prison in someone, and they have reason to kill again. I don't want to hear anyone climbing Megan's frame about this case. You come try climbing mine instead." Ryan looked at everyone, then sat down.

The bookstore was so silent that Megan could hear each individual breathing. Everyone flinched when Herb Jackson III pushed back his folding chair and stood up. "I echo everything Ryan said, and I'm ashamed that I didn't say it first. Megan, I apologize for my tardiness."

There were embarrassed voices muttering apologies, and no one would meet her eyes except Ray Roberts, and he had supported her. Megan stood up and looked around the circle. "Everyone get over the embarrassment or shame or whatever emotion everyone feels. We don't have the time to waste on petty disagreements. The murderer has gotten away with his crime for five years, and I don't want him to spend another day at liberty."

She handed a small stack of papers to Ryan to pass out. She waited until everyone had their copy of a list of suspects containing a brief biography and their relationship to Jessica Murphy. "The problem with a case this old is alibis. Since no one knows exactly when Jessica was murdered, only the time Gray Wolf Murphy reported her missing, there is no way to check alibis. Sam Reece and Bill Owens are self-employed, and Gray Wolf is, too. The museum doesn't keep attendance records on their curators, so I can't prove or disprove Dr. Ryland's alibi. Gray Wolf reported

Jessica missing on September twenty-fourth five years ago, but he was out of town from September twentieth to twenty-third. He could have killed her before he left town or after he got back. Any of the suspects could have killed her during the time Gray Wolf was out of town. So everyone had opportunity. Sex or money are the two most prevalent motives. We don't have a hint that Jessica had any big bucks, so sex it is."

Megan tucked a curl behind her ear, knowing that it would slip back against her cheek the minute her head turned. She smiled at Ryan, took a breath, and continued. "The weapon has not been found, and given the length of time since the murder and the discovery of the body, the knife could have been cleaned of blood ten times over, not that anybody can get all of the blood off a knife. Or the knife could have been thrown in the Canadian River, although I don't think that's a good option given the fact that the river has only an inch or two of water ninety percent of the time. The point is that anything could have happened to it. The only thing I know for sure is that it was most likely a broad blade, pointed, with only one edge sharpened. Both Gray Wolf and Sam Reece have large knife collections. Lieutenant Carr has booked both collections into evidence to be checked for blood, which surely Gray Wolf's will have, since they're Comanche artifacts. If blood is found, the DNA testing will take from several days to several weeks to several months depending on how many knives are checked. Not that it matters who has a collection of knives. Jessica could have been killed with an ordinary kitchen knife one uses to chop onions."

"So there you have it, for what it's worth," said Megan, sitting back and sipping her coffee which was now cold.

"I read all of Aaron Elkins's books this last week, but I

didn't find any hints that would help on this case," said Lorene.

"I read two of Kathy Reich's books about the forensic anthropologist, but I didn't find that they helped," said Candi Hobbs.

"Are you sure there wasn't something special about the nicks in the ribs and vertebra that would be a clue?" asked Agnes. "Dr. Gideon Oliver always finds a special clue."

"Dr. Gideon Oliver is welcome to come down and look at Jessica's skeleton, but he'll find no more than I did," retorted Megan.

"I don't think another anthropologist on the scene would be helpful. This Dr. Oliver may be great, but I'm going to guess that he's no better than Megan," said Ryan. Megan saw that puzzled look on his face he always got when he made some totally wrong remark and everyone stared at him.

"Hush, Ryan, before you stick your foot in your mouth again and choke on it," whispered Megan.

Ryan looked puzzled.

The bell tinkled over the bookstore door as Lieutenant Jerry Carr walked in. "I'm against a charade with a suspected murderer," he said, striding over to the couch to stand in front of Megan.

Megan rubbed her bare arms where goose bumps appeared. "If there was any other way to do this, I'd take it."

"Hey, what's going on? What are you two talking about?" demanded Ryan, looking as belligerent as Megan imagined he would be.

"This case is so old that we can't check alibis, provided anyone could remember where he was five years ago. We have no eyewitnesses, and we have no weapon. In short, the only thing we have is my logical analysis."

"Does that mean you've solved the case, Megan?" asked Candi, blinking furiously. She had exchanged her glasses for contacts last spring but didn't seem to tolerate them well. Megan figured that if Candi could stand the blinking, so could she.

"I think so, but Jerry told me last night that we couldn't prove it. We have no evidence at all. So our only hope is a confession, and after five years I don't think we can rely on the murderer's conscience to give us one voluntarily."

"When did you talk to him last night about confessions? When I was with you the lieutenant was doing a good job of chewing us up and spitting us out? You're going to do something dangerous, aren't you, Megan? And you," said Ryan, getting off the couch and walking up the to the lieutenant. He poked Jerry Carr in the chest with his finger. "And you are going to let her do it. She's not a cop. You've got other police officers, use them."

"I can't," said Jerry. "It has to be someone the suspect knows or the plan won't work."

"What plan?" shouted Ryan.

"Ryan, calm down. I'll be fine. After we get the pertinent information on tape—"

"Tape! Tape? You're going to go wired to interview someone?" Ryan's voice was loud, almost a shout and Megan flinched.

"There's no other way, Ryan. I either trick her into a confession on tape, or she walks. I don't want her getting a free pass on this murder. By killing Jessica Murphy, she changed several lives and none of them for the good."

"I won't let you go," said Ryan.

"You can't stop me."

"Leave her alone, Doc. We need her. We'll be listening; we won't let anything happen to her."

"Where will you be, Lieutenant? You've seen those

houses on the rim of Sunday Canyon. You can't park the Special Crimes van or police cars anywhere near them, there's no place inconspicuous. For God's sake, it's just one street. It's a long one as streets go since it runs along the canyon rim, but trust me on this one, the minute any strange car crosses that cattle guard north of that community, everybody will know."

"We'll set up at Bill Owens' house, in his living room, in fact. That's across the street—road, rather—and down one house."

"Did you say 'she,' Megan?" asked Agnes. "Which one of these woman do you think did it?"

She looked at Jerry Carr, and he nodded his head. "Go ahead. I don't think any of them will get on the phone and tattle to her. Or the media. Anybody that calls the paper or the television stations will be sorry. I'll make his or her life so miserable, there aren't words to describe it."

"Think of all the mysteries about skeletons and forensic anthropologists. Jessica's body was found more or less sitting up in a shallow grave. All the bones were there. What is wrong with that picture?" asked Megan, looking around the circle of club members.

"The skeleton was sitting up," said Agnes. "But there's no reason to bury a body sitting up."

"All the bones were there, and they shouldn't be. The animals that dug up the grave should have carried off the bones like your dogs did," said Candi.

"If there were no bones missing, that must mean that the skeleton was exposed just before you found it, Megan," said Rosemary.

"And it was exposed by a person because all the bones were there," said Randel, preening at his brilliant guesswork.

"And it was deliberately arranged in a sitting position," said Lorene. "I think so it would be more noticeable."

"Who exposed it?" asked Megan.

"The murderer," said Ray Roberts. "No one else would know where it was."

"Why was it exposed?" asked Megan.

"Because the murderer wanted it found," said Ryan. "And I know who it is and why she killed Jessica Murphy."

20

They'll tell you that the most destructive force in the world is hate. Don't you believe it, lad. It's love. And if you want to make a detective you'd better learn to recognize it when you meet it.

—Chief Superintendent Adam Dalgleish, quoting old Greenall, the first detective-sergeant he had worked under, in P. D. James's *Death of an Expert Witness,* 1977

LITTLE SUNDAY CANYON, PRESENT DAY

I wish I had carried through on my threat to Megan. I wish I had locked her in the basement during the day and handcuffed her to my bed at night. I would read her Westerns by Ernest Haycox and Dorothy M. Johnson. I think I would choose Haycox's *Bugles in the Afternoon* first. That's one of the best novels about Custer and the Battle of the Little Bighorn. And almost any short story by Johnson is a good choice, although I'm biased in favor of "The Man Who Shot Liberty Valance," and "A Man Called Horse." Best of all, Megan would never be in danger again. Except maybe from me. Maybe I'd better not handcuff her to the bed. I don't trust my strength of character that far.

But I didn't lock her in my basement this morning, so I ended up sitting behind Indian Rock, sweating with fear and praying that my headphones would pick up Megan's voice without shorting out. Jerry Carr had her wired up six ways to Sunday. I peeked around the rock at approximately the place where Randel was crouching under the balcony. Ray Roberts was crouching opposite Randel on the other side beneath the balcony. Herb and half the SWAT team were across the stream hidden in the trees behind me. The women of Murder by the Yard were waiting in Bill Owens' living room. The book club women and the cops had crawled through the pasture behind Bill Owens' house. I heard Jerry Carr got caught on a barbed wire fence. It broke my heart to learn of his mishap.

I had a bad premonition about this plan, so in addition to sweating, my stomach was burning up. The moon was full and bright enough to read a book by its light. You could see pretty well everything you needed to see, but the moon cast shadows, too, so it was eerie around Indian Rock, particularly since I kept remembering there were two empty graves within spitting distance of where I was sitting. I kept creeping down to a plum thicket about ten feet away to relieve myself until I stepped on a rock and twisted my ankle. I swore I would never drink coffee before a stakeout again.

I heard Megan's voice through my earphones.

"Hello, Peggy, I hope you don't mind my inviting myself to dinner, but I thought we might as well mix food with questions." I heard the door close and two sets of footsteps.

"I'm just glad to see you again. I'm so curious. Have you found out anything yet? Which one of the suspects is guilty? I'll put my money on Anita Reece even if she is a little loose in the head. There's nothing in her attic but some dust, so to speak."

There was a clatter of dishes, then I heard Megan's voice again. "I'll fix the salad, Peggy. I brought all kinds of crunchy veggies and two different kinds of lettuce."

"No, not that knife!" Peggy's voice very loud with a touch of panic. "I only use it to cut meat. Take another knife."

"You must not eat meat very often, Peggy. This knife is greasy and dusty. I don't think you've washed it since you stabbed Jessica Murphy. I can't imagine why you kept it unless you didn't want to break up the set in that cute little knife holder."

"Give me that knife!" Peggy's voice, sounding manic.

"Get out of there, Megan," I kept whispering, but she stayed with the script. She was calm as could be—or scared numb.

"This knife is broad-bladed, pointed, and sharpened on one edge just like the one that made the nicks in Jessica's vertebra. You know what? You are a very clever woman. Dr. Stevens and I came out here looking for someone who knew all the participants and could provide information. You described Jessica as promiscuous, but no one else did. It wasn't until I realized that most of the information that I had on the case came from you, that I thought how different the case would be if Jessica was just a friendly woman. Then no one would have a motive except you. Why didn't you wait out the seven years, Peggy? Why disturb the grave so Jessica's remains would be found? If you had been patient, no one would ever know what happened to Jessica. It was very stupid of you, Peggy."

"I hated her and the way she treated Gray Wolf. I killed her and seduced him. I knew I had committed the perfect crime. But seven years is so long. And Gray Wolf was talking about selling his house and moving to Oklahoma. That's where all the Comanches live. I couldn't take a chance that he wouldn't ask me along and he wouldn't unless we were married. He felt such terrible guilt. Now, give me that knife."

Every muscle in my body was stiff. I have never been so afraid in my life. Then I heard Megan's voice again and she didn't sound calm any more.

"I think I'll keep the knife. I've never liked the idea of being stabbed."

"That's all right. I'll shoot you instead. I ordered a silencer from one of those survivalist magazines. You never know when you might need something like this."

"I see you plan ahead, Peggy. I want to ask you something since we're having this nice conversation. You told me you liked to keep your eyes on things. Is that why you buried Jessica just under your own house, so you could keep an eye on her? Were you afraid she would crawl out of her grave?"

"Don't be ridiculous. Now, give me that knife!" Peggy was screaming now. And I was ready to throw the plan to the wind and climb up that balcony and throw that sick woman off it.

"Yes, let's go out on the balcony, so when I shoot you, I can just tip you over. When it gets late, after midnight, I'll climb down and bury you. Jessica's grave will do. The dirt is still loose, so no one will think that there's another body buried there."

There was a scream, then I heard something or someone crashing through the juniper and all the other scratchy vegetation. I peered around Indian Rock and saw Megan crashing down the slope.

"Come back here, you bitch!" Peggy Otlander's voice bounced off the canyon walls.

I saw her sturdy body climbing over the balcony rail. I saw Randel and Ray Roberts raise up and move slowly toward a spot midway under the balcony.

"Megan!" I whispered as loud as I could.

"Ryan? She has a gun with a silencer. She'll kill me." She stumbled into my arms.

I looked around, desperate to find a hiding place. I didn't want to run for the trees across the stream. Bullets travel faster than I can run. Then I saw what was our only hope of avoiding bullet holes in our gizzards or wherever if Randel and Ray didn't tackle Peggy. "The rock, honey," I said. "Let me boost you up." I laced my fingers together to provide a step up.

"You're a genius, Ryan. Let me be the mother of your children."

I dropped Megan on her behind.

"What happened, Ryan. Are you hurt? You have that weak wrist from falling off the cliff when we went rock climbing."

"I'm fine," I mumbled and boosted her up on top of the rock. Just as I scrambled on top of Indian Rock myself, I heard some curses and a gun going off. I looked toward the balcony in time to see Randal and Ray collide in the dark and fall. They rolled down the slope, passing Indian Rock at a fair clip. Peggy Otlander kept firing at them as she started down the incline. The SWAT team hiding in the trees behind us cut loose with what sounded like mortars. I hoped to hell that they saw Megan and me on top of the rock. Surely they had night-vision goggles, but in case they didn't I threw myself on top of Megan to act as a human shield. I heard a whoosh like air escaping from a bicycle, and Megan began squirming beneath me.

"Lie still, Megan!" I hissed in her ear. "Quit wiggling or she'll hear us moving around." If I hadn't been scared spitless and past forty; if there hadn't been gunfire echoing off the high rock walls of the canyon; if there hadn't been a pissed off, psychotic woman with a gun hunting for us; and if Megan and I had been alone in that intimate position, I might have made an overtly sexual move on my redhead. However, circumstances being what they were, I didn't even think of it until several hours later.

Meanwhile, I lifted my head just enough to see over the edge of the rock. I caught a glimpse of Peggy zigzagging down the slope in a duck walk. She must have stepped on a rock like I did, because I saw her feet go up in the air and she slid down the slope on her back, grabbing without success for bushes to slow herself down. She hit the rock at an angle. I heard a sharp crack and figured she had broken something. It wasn't her skull because she kept cursing.

She limped to the back of the rock, her left arm hanging uselessly at her side. She scrabbled at the side of the rock, trying to climb up after us. "You rotten slut! Interfering in my business! I'm gonna rip your head off and feed you to the hogs!"

I rolled off Megan. "Move!" I whispered, grabbing her arm to pull her along with me to the opposite edge of the rock from Peggy. I heard Megan sucking in air, and wondered why she was so breathless. Terror, probably.

"Don't worry, honey. I don't think she owns any hogs." I heard Megan making little hissing sounds.

I really hate to write about the conclusion to our stakeout and Megan's attempt to trick Peggy. Parental discretion is advised for this next scene. Anyway, after Megan and Special Crimes had dug up two graves we should have guessed that Indian Rock had been undermined. Add Peggy's attempts to climb up the side opposite the two graves, and the rock was seriously unstable. I felt it begin to wobble, then tilt, and I yelled at Megan to jump. Peggy may have been strong, but she wasn't agile and her reflexes were not quick. To summarize, Indian Rock began to roll, and Peggy turned and began to run, only she didn't angle her path away from the huge rock. She screamed once, a shrill sound full of mindless terror.

By the time Megan and I picked ourselves off the ground to look at our murderer, Peggy looked as if she had been run through a very large wringer.

I claimed that it was Jessica's revenge, but Megan disagreed. "Jessica wasn't a vengeful person in life, and I doubt that she would be any different in death. No, Ryan, we have to look further afield than Jessica. We have to look for someone who was enraged that Peggy's callous disrespect for the dead disturbed their rest."

"Gray Wolf? Peggy certainly disturbed his wife's rest."

"Jessica Murphy was not the only woman buried at Indian Rock."

I felt a chill prickle my skin. "Megan, Miss Comanche has been dead for a minium of 130 years, maybe more. There's no one left alive to be enraged."

"Miss Comanche was a most-beloved woman. Don't you believe the spirit of her lover would return to watch over her resting place? Don't you believe love transcends the grave?"

EPILOGUE
1868

*You don't have much hope of getting the truth, if you
think you know in advance what the truth ought to be.*

—Spenser in Robert B. Parker's
Pale Kings and Princes, 1987

PALO DURO CANYON

*It was several weeks before Spotted Tongue felt lonely for
his friends. It was that long before he decided that he
would live, if for no other reason than he refused to lie on a
travois to travel with the Nermernuh. Next week he would
ride the white mare now that she had delivered her foal.
But today he would eat buffalo with his friends.*

*"Green Willow told Topay that you would soon be cured
because your temper was quick these last few days," said
Shaking Hand.*

*Wild Horse grasped Spotted Tongue's hand. "I'm glad
you will live. I would not want to live with the sorrow I felt
after we fought."*

*Spotted Tongue thought Wild Horse looked sorrowful, but
he still did not trust him. He had been too quick to deny Spotted Tongue help when he needed information. "I am glad we
did not fight to the death for I would hate to carry the sorrow
of killing you," said Spotted Tongue with a smile.*

Wild Horse laughed. "I would be the one carrying sorrow, Spotted Tongue."

Fat Belly grasped his friend's hand. "Green Willow said you knew that Buffalo Woman murdered Little Flower before she tried to kill you. Tell us how you knew."

"I knew whoever murdered Little Flower hoped to gain from her death. None of you would gain, but only lose. Buffalo Woman wanted to be my second wife. She hated Little Flower, whom she blamed for my failure to take her as my wife. Then when she learned Little Flower carried my child, Buffalo Woman knew I would never cast her away. So Buffalo Woman killed her, hoping that I would replace Little Flower with her as my second wife. But I had already decided that I would not. She tried to kill me when she heard me say that I needed to talk to Topay again."

"What did my wife tell you?" asked Shaking Hand. "She did not see Buffalo Woman kill Little Flower or she would have told me first."

"But Topay didn't have to see Buffalo Woman pick up that rock and kill Little Flower to know what she did. You see, Topay told me she sat down and waited until she could no longer hear Deer Fawn. She did not say that Buffalo Woman waited with her, and since she saw no one walking down the path toward the plum thickets, she believed she did not see the murderer. But Topay didn't think of the murderer as someone behind her. According to Slow Like a Turtle, Buffalo Woman walked along the path toward camp with her. But Topay says that Buffalo Woman walked with her. Would Topay lie? I do not believe that she did. Did Slow Like a Turtle lie? I do not believe that she did, anymore than I believe Topay did. Why should they lie? They do not want to share my tipi as one of my wives. But Buffalo Woman did. So she had something to gain. Also, Buffalo Woman walked out

of that canyon twice. Once with Slow Like a Turtle, once with Topay. Why did she do that? To return to kill Little Flower. By the time she returned, killed Little Flower, and came up the path behind Topay, there was no one left alive in that canyon. Green Willow had walked out first, then Buffalo Woman with Slow Like a Turtle, leaving behind Deer Fawn because she complained to much. No one wants to listen to her. But she is too big and awkward and clumsy to kill Little Flower. She would make more noise than a buffalo caught in a plum thicket. Little Flower would hear her before Deer Fawn could sneak up and hit her in the back of her head. And again I ask, what did Deer Fawn have to gain? She is already Wild Horse's wife and carries his son, and Wild Horse has nearly as many ponies as I do."

"If she was not carrying my son, I would pay you ponies to take her," said Wild Horse. "She talks all the time unless she is asleep, and sometimes even then. Soon I will have no more sense in my head than Buffalo Woman's mother."

"It will not be a long wait," said Fat Belly, punching Wild Horse's arm. Wild Horse hit him back, and the two rolled in the dirt like small boys.

Spotted Tongue felt many winters older than Wild Horse and Fat Belly. Without medicine he must protect himself and hide his thoughts from the People. That left little time to ease himself by playing with his friends. "Stop! Do you want to hear more about Buffalo Woman?"

Wild Horse and Fat Belly untangled themselves and sat up. "Go on, Spotted Tongue, tell us more. We will not fight until you finish your story."

"Buffalo Woman does not have a brother or a father to hunt for her, so what meat they have that I do not give them, Buffalo Woman hunts and kills. She can sneak up on

*a buffalo or a deer nearly as well as a man. Little Flower
would not have heard her."*

"She killed for you?" said Fat Belly. "She was desperate.
There are many better-looking warriors than you."

"But not more ponies than Spotted Tongue," said Shaking Hand. "He can trade ponies with the Comancheros for
anything his wives want."

"My loss was love, and she hoped to gain love. It balanced out," said Spotted Tongue. "But the best part of the
story is what Green Willow did. She saw me fall and Buffalo Woman standing over me, and she grabbed the cook
pot that I traded for with the Comancheros. I got it for Little Flower, so her spirit took revenge through the cook pot.
She was a woman above others. Both my wives are."

EPILOGUE

PRESENT DAY

The most incredible thing about miracles is that they happen.

—"The Blue Cross," in G. K. Chesterton's
The Innocence of Father Brown, 1911

PALO DURO CANYON

"It's done," said Megan, propping her shovel against Indian Rock. She looked at Ryan and attempted to decipher his expression. It wasn't pensive exactly, maybe thoughtful would be a better description. His face was certainly somber. But at least he didn't appear angry. She had prepared herself for his disapproval and exasperation at the least, furious anger and refusal as the worst scenario. No, that wasn't right. The worst scenario would have been his calling 911 from the morgue and telling the police that Dr. Megan Clark, Ph.D., was stealing the mummy known as Miss Comanche.

"Ryan, why did you agree to help me reinter Miss Comanche in her grave? I didn't expect you to, at least I didn't expect you to without a major, major argument."

He stuffed his hands in the back pockets of his Levis. "Did you ever discover her real name?"

"It's Miss Comanche."

He turned his head and looked at her. "I'm serious,

Megan. Has your research turned up a candidate for the position of Comanche Captive?"

Megan drew circles in the dust with her sandals. "I found an account of a young woman from Parker County—Parker County seemed to be a favorite target of Comanche raids—who was carried away after witnessing the murder of her husband and two-year-old son. A fourteen-year-old cousin was hiding in the branches of a tall oak tree and saw everything that happened. The reason I'm fairly certain this is our mummy is the fact that the account in Wilbarger's book describes the woman as being very tall, five-ten in fact. That would be tall today, but in 1868 she was a giantess. According to my calculations Miss Comanche would have been five feet, ten inches tall."

"What was her name?"

Megan looked up at him. "Miss Comanche."

"Megan, come on, tell me."

"I did, Ryan. She has no family left in Texas that I could find. Her young cousin was killed the next year in another Comanche raid. And I don't think she would want to be buried by her husband and child—provided we could find their graves. She was five months pregnant with the child of a Comanche warrior. If she had been rescued instead of murdered, she would have borne the stigma the rest of her life. It wasn't fair, but it was the way things were. No, for good or not so good, our mummy was a Comanche who was well loved. I think it's better she stay here in Palo Duro Canyon where she was loved than be returned to rest among those who would have looked askance at her had she returned to Parker County."

"You're not going to tell me her name, are you?"

"No, because she was not that person when she died. I'm sure she didn't ask for her life to be changed so severely, but life doesn't ask us what would suit us best." She picked up the shovel. "Let's go home, Ryan. I'm sad and I need to watch a movie with you, something funny, please."

He clasped her hand and they started down the trail when she heard a voice. She jerked away from Ryan and whirled around. The leaves on the plum bushes hung motionless and the canyon was utterly quiet. The air shimmered by Indian Rock, and just for a moment, a split second that Megan only remembered when she returned to Palo Duro Canyon, she thought she saw a tall young woman in a white buckskin dress holding hands with a Comanche warrior in breech-clout and moccasins. Both were smiling.

"Megan, what were you waving at?" asked Ryan, looking back at Indian Rock with a puzzled expression.

"I was waving at Miss Comanche."

"If you say so."

Megan smiled.